SO YOU THINK YOU KNOW

Test Cricket?

A division of Hodder Headline Limited

© Hodder Children's Books 2005
Published in Great Britain in 2005
by Hodder Children's Books
Editor: Paula Borton
Design by Andrew Summers
Cover design: Hodder Children's Books

2

A catalogue record for this book is available from the British Library

ISBN-10: 0340902930
ISBN-13: 9780340902936

Printed by Bookmarque Ltd, Croydon, Surrey

The paper and board used in this paperback by Hodder Children's Books are natural recyclable products made from wood grown in sustainable forests. The manufacturing processes conform to the environmental regulations of the country of origin.

Hodder Children's Books
a division of Hodder Headline Limited
338 Euston Road
London NW1 3BH

Contents

Introduction   v

Cricket quizzes   7

Sticky wicket (tricky questions)   133

Answers   140

Introduction

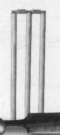

So you think you know Test Match cricket?
Think you can remember all of the great
performances and characters? Reckon you can
recall all the marvellous matches, grounds and
individuals that have made the game as
fascinating and compelling as it is? Then this
is the book for you.

Contained within its pages are 1,050
questions on all aspects of Test Cricket, as well
as some questions on the One Day
International scene and the World Cups. The
questions run up to the beginning of
December 2004 and extend far back into
history and to the formation of Test-playing
sides and competitions. I hope you enjoy
tackling the questions as much as I did
researching and compiling them.

About the Author

Clive Gifford is an experienced writer and journalist with more than 60 books in print. These include most of the *So You Think You Know* series and many sports books including *Super Activ: Cricket – a coaching guide for young players, The Making Of A Champion Sprinter, Drugs And Sport* and the award-winning *Football: The Ultimate Guide To The Beautiful Game.* Clive was an enthusiastic, if none too proficient, junior cricketer whose greatest claim to fame was bowling Mike Brearley in the nets during the England captain's school visit. He now contents himself with watching the game as often as possible.

Many thanks to Travis Basevi for his expert guidance.

1. Two English batsmen scored centuries in each innings of a Test Match in 2004. Can you name them?

2. Between which two sides were the Victory Tests held in 1945?

3. Who is the only Pakistan player to take two hat-tricks of wickets in Test Matches?

4. Which current Australian cricketer's first six wickets of his Test Match career were all taken in one innings, with figures of 6 for 9?

5. Which England batsman had a perfect winning record as captain in the 1970s of the One Day International side?

6. From which country does international umpire, Brent 'Billy' Bowden come?

7. Which early Test Cricketer from England took a staggering 112 wickets at just 10.75 each in 18 matches before dying of tuberculosis: Archie MacLaren, George Lohmann or George Hirst?

8. Which side had four of its players run out in the 1975 World Cup Final?

9. Who broke his left thumb in a 1984 test and batted with a cast on, before then taking seven wickets for 53?

10. Which ground has hosted the most One Day Internationals?

11. Which father and son both made centuries on their Test Match debuts for India?

12. Which Australian captain was the first cricketer to take seven catches as a fielder in a Test Match?

13. Who with a top score of below 70 was the top scorer in the entire Fourth Test between India and Australia in 2004?

14. In the early 1970s, which team played in 10 consecutive drawn Test Matches?

15. What sort of aircraft did David Gower fly when he buzzed his team mates on the ground during the 1991 Ashes tour?

16. Who was the first black captain of the West Indies for more than a single match?

17. In which country was the first World Cup competition held?

18. Only four English counties were represented in the England team that played in the very first Test Match. Yorkshire was one – can you name two of the others?

19. In the 1890s, the English Test side was chosen by the county on whose ground the match was to be held: true or false?

20. How many Test Matches have been played as of the end of 2004: over 1,100, over 1,350, over 1,500 or over 1,700?

21. Which team has scored the highest total in a Test Match?

22. Which Australian is the leading Test wicket-taker at the Sharjah Stadium with 16 wickets?

23. In which country would you be if you were watching Test cricket at Eden Park?

24. What position did Donald Bradman bat when he scored his 304 against England in 1934?

25. In 2004, who hit a six into the grandstand where his father attempted to catch, but dropped the ball?

26. Which fast bowler is the only West Indian to have played in a 100 Test Matches?

27. Which side in 2002 scored 451 runs in the final innings of a Test Match and still lost?

28. Which player has hit the most sixes in One Day Internationals?

29. In 1982, which Australian bowler dislocated his shoulder and was out for more than a season after he tackled a pitch invader at the WACA ground?

30. Zaheer Abbas scored a century in each innings of a first class match once, three or eight times?

31. Which side recorded the lowest One Day International total in 2004 when they were bowled out by Sri Lanka for 35?

32. In the 1981 Headingley Test, were Bob Willis's match-winning figures: 7-43, 8-42, 7-49 or 8-43?

33. Against which side did Ian Botham record his best-ever bowling figures of 8-34?

34. Which Test Match cricket ground staged the 1988 Rugby Union World Cup Final?

35. Which West Indian batsman scored 8,540 runs in Test Matches, a further 6,721 in One Day International matches and also played in World Cup Football qualifications?

36. Which England batsman was nicknamed, 'The Judge'?

37. Which West Indian fast bowler took 6 for 3 against Bangladesh in 2003: Fidel Edwards, Jermaine Lawson or Tino Best?

38. Which English fast bowler, with the middle name, Augustine, published two volumes of poetry?

39. Whose debut as a Test umpire in 1992–93 and as a One Day International umpire both occurred at the Port Elizabeth cricket ground in South Africa?

40. Who scored a triple century for India in their mammoth total of 675-5 in the First Test v Pakistan in 2004?

41. Which West Indian player has a Test batting average at the Queen's Park Oval of 97.64: Viv Richards, Everton Weekes, Brian Lara or Chris Gayle?

42. Which England fast bowler took 325 Test wickets but never took 10 wickets in a match?

43. Which former New Zealand cricketer's father had captained New Zealand, his brother had played for New Zealand and his wife, Karen, had played for the New Zealand women's team?

44. Against which side did Sri Lanka notch up an incredible 952 runs in an innings before declaring?

45. The 1932–33 Bodyline Tour was broadcast to England from a studio located in the Eiffel Tower in Paris: true or false?

46. Which team holds a 100% record against Pakistan in cricket's World Cup?

47. Which Australian spinner has taken over 150 Test wickets, has a One Day International batting average of 1.00 and has the middle names, Charles Glyndwr?

48. Which Sri Lankan batsman made a pair of ducks on his debut, but went on to score more than 10 Test Match centuries?

49. Who was the only Englishman to make it into the ICC's Team of the Year for 2004?

50. In which match as England captain did Ray Illingworth suffer his first defeat: 4th, 9th, 13th or 20th?

1. Which England batsman and captain twice made Test Match scores of 157 at the Oval, London?

2. Who has the first and second best-ever Test Match bowling figures at Old Trafford, and obtained them both in the same match?

3. In the 2003–04 Test Series between Australia and India who top-scored with 305 runs in one match?

4. Who has captained England in the most One Day Internationals?

5. In the inaugural World Cup, who managed to beat India by a massive 202-run winning margin?

6. Which great West Indian cricketer had a batting average of over 85 against both Pakistan and India, but only 22 against New Zealand?

7. Against which side did Shoaib Akhtar take six wickets in 8.2 overs for just 11 runs in 2002?

8. By how many runs did England win the legendary 1981 Headingley Test against Australia?

9. What is the most runs ever scored in a single Test Match: 1,121, 1,508, 1,799 or 1,981?

10. Which team has won the most consecutive Test series: England, Australia or Pakistan?

11. Which Pakistan player made a century and took 11 wickets in a Test against India in 1982–83?

12. Against which opposing side did Australia's Mark Waugh score more of his Test Match runs?

13. Who was the first Indian Test cricketer to play in the Sheffield Shield in Australia?

14. Who has made more Test Match appearances for England than any other player?

15. The same English player became Curtly Ambrose's 200th, 250th and 400th Test victim. Who was he?

16. In terms of matches, what is the name of New Zealand's longest serving captain?

17. Whose highest Test score of 128 not out came against the Australians in the 1989 Ashes series?

18. Does Aravinda de Silva, Arjuna Ranatunga or Sanath Jayasuriya hold the Sri Lankan Test Match record for the highest innings?

19. Which English county had Shoaib Ahktar and Herschel Gibbs as its overseas players in 2003?

20. Which US President was the first to witness a Test Match?

21. Who scored nine One Day International hundreds and a record total of 1,894 One Day International runs in 1998?

22. Trent Bridge has held 19 Ashes Test Matches. Have England won 3, 8, 11 or 14 of these matches?

23. Who took four wickets to leave India 0 for 4 in a 1952 Test Match against England?

24. Who captained South Africa in their first Test Match after their 1992 return to Test Cricket?

25. Which Pakistan all-rounder has batted in every position from number 3 to number 11 in One Day Internationals?

26. Who scored 177 at Adelaide in 2002: Michael Vaughan, Damien Martyn or Justin Langer?

27. How many over 50-year-olds have played Test cricket for England?

28. Which Pakistan spin bowler's best figures were 9 for 56 against England in 1987?

29. Can you name either of the opening batsmen for Australia who both made double centuries in the same innings of a Test, the only instance of this occurring?

30. Which Pakistan spin bowler in 2003 became the first bowler in five years to take 100 wickets in English county cricket?

31. Ashley Giles' best bowling performance in One Day Internationals is 5-57. Is this better, worse or the same as his best bowling performance in Test Matches?

32. Which Sri Lankan cricketer has scored over 2,000 Test runs, but has yet to make a century?

33. Sydney Barnes took a record 38, 43 or 49 wickets in a Test series?

34. How many Yorkshiremen played in the very first Test Match for England?

35. Who is the only bowler to take more than 100 Test wickets at a single cricket ground?

36. How many overs a side were played in the 1975 World Cup matches?

37. Other than retired out, stumped, caught, LBW, bowled and run out, can you name three of the other ways in which a batsman can be out?

38. Was Waqar Younis, Wasim Akram or Shoaib Akhtar the only Pakistan player to take four Test wickets in five balls?

39. Who retired hurt after scoring 165 runs in the very first Test Match?

40. Which Englishman took 23 Test wickets in a 118-Test-Match career?

41. Which English fast bowler was such an admirer of Bob Dylan that he added Dylan as a middle name?

42. Who was the first Pakistan Test batsman to hit 100 centuries in his first-class career?

43. Who scored a stunning 189 not out versus England at Old Trafford in 1984?

44. Who succeeded Allan Border as captain of Australia: Mark Taylor, Mark Waugh or Mark Slater?

45. Who won the very first One Day International match?

46. Which team managed to win 5-0 in two Test Match series against England in the mid-1980s?

47. At which English Test ground did Glenn McGrath torment England in 1997, taking 8-38 in one innings?

48. How many times in his 52 Test Matches did Mushtaq Ahmed take five wickets in an innings?

49. For which English county did Ian Botham play and help win two County Championships after leaving Somerset?

50. In which country would you find the Tyrone Fernando Stadium?

1. Who was captain of England on the infamous 'Bodyline' tour?

2. Have there been 45, 60, 75 or 90 Test Match grounds?

3. Who top-scored for the West Indies with 105 during West Indies successful fourth innings chase of 418 set by Australia in 2003?

4. Who took 53 Test wickets in 11 Test Matches while Shane Warne was banned for a year?

5. Charles Fleetwood-Smith holds the dubious record of conceding more runs as a bowler in a Test Match innings than any other player. Did he concede 197, 218, 234 or 298?

6. Who was dropped by the Australians in 1992 after his first two Test Matches only yielded one wicket?

7. Which Pakistan leg spinner bowls left-handed, bats right handed and succeeded Abdul Qadir as Pakistan's main leg spin bowler?

8. Which Indian cricketer's batting average was 100.37 in the calendar year, 2003?

9. Which ground became England's eighth Test Match venue in 2003?

10. Two South Africans made it into the ICC's 2004 Team of the Year? Can you name them?

11. What was the last year in which England won an Ashes Test held at Lord's?

12. Which 2002–03 World Cup team's innings against Australia saw extras top score with 15, one third of the entire total?

13. South Africa recorded the lowest ever aggregate runs in a Test Match. Did they score a total of 48, 81, 99 or 106?

14. How many times has a batsman made 114 in a Test Match in England?

15. Of the 20 leading Test Match wicketkeepers by dismissals, does Ian Healy, Adam Parore, Godfrey Evans or Alan Knott hold the record for the most stumpings with 46?

16. Wisden's five Cricketers of the Century contained two Australians. Can you name them?

17. Whose selection for a tour of South Africa eventually resulted in the tour being cancelled and South Africa outlawed from international cricket?

18. Who became a Test-Match-playing nation first: West Indies, Sri Lanka or India?

19. In the legendary Fifth Test of the 1968 Ashes series, who took four wickets in just 27 balls to bowl out Australia?

20. New Zealander, Shayne O'Connor was Shaun Pollock, Allan Donald or Courtney Walsh's 300th Test wicket?

21. Which South African was the only player in 2003 to be banned from a period of playing One Day Internationals and Test Matches?

22. Who is the only player to have scored over 1,000 Test runs at the Trent Bridge cricket ground?

23. In the 1992 World Cup, Zimbabwe scored 312 but were beaten by which side?

24. Did Alec Stewart or his father, Micky, have a higher batting average in Tests against Pakistan?

25. Who were the two captains during the 1968 Ashes series?

26. Who was born in Australia, played in the infamous 'Bodyline' Ashes series for England and became England's Chairman of Selectors in 1955?

27. Of the all-time top ten wicket-takers, who has the lowest average: Shane Warne, Anil Kumble or Curtly Ambrose?

28. Who through two unbeaten innings of 274 and 69 remained on the field for all bar 44 minutes of the 2003 First Test between Sri Lanka and New Zealand?

29. In the 1992–93 tour of India, which single player was England's leading wicket-taker, run-scorer and catcher in the Test Matches?

30. Which Asian cricket ground has a fort at one end and a view overlooking the Indian Ocean at the other?

31. Can you name the one batsman still playing who is in England's list of top ten all-time leading Test run scorers?

32. Russell Endean's dismissal in a 1956–57 South Africa versus England Test was the first of what type of dismissal in Test cricket?

33. Who made 107 consecutive appearances for Australia between 1993 and 2002?

34. Which English bowler holds the record for the most Test Match wickets taken at Headingley?

35. Which Indian batsman batted throughout a 60-over-a-side match against England in the 1975 World Cup yet only made 36?

36. Which cricket trophy became the permanent trophy from 1999, was made by the Queen's jewellers, Garrard's, weighs 11 kg and features a golden globe held aloft by three pillars representing the stumps?

37. Who took the most dismissals (catching and stumping) in Test Matches as a wicketkeeper for England?

38. Which bowler made his England debut at the age of 33 versus South Africa: Neil Foster, Joey Benjamin or Richard Johnson?

39. Did Dudley Nourse, Eddie Barlow or Peter Pollock once score 208 runs in an innings against England while nursing a broken thumb?

40. Which New Zealand batsman became the first to pass 4,000 Test runs for his country?

41. Who was the first West Indian to take a hat trick in Test cricket: Wes Hall, Charlie Griffiths, Michael Holding or Andy Roberts?

42. On what ground was the first-ever Test Match held?

43. Which cricketing legend became the first batsman to make 8,000 Test runs?

44. Which New Zealander scored 64 off 21 balls in a 2004 One Day International match: Chris Cairns, Daniel Vettori or Craig McMillan?

45. Who is the only Englishman to have scored 1,000 runs and taken 100 wickets in One Day International cricket?

46. Who defeated England in the final of the ICC Champions Trophy in 2004?

47. Who was the first batsman to score seven Test hundreds in a single calendar year?

48. Can you name two of Ian Botham's three partners as he steered England from 135 for 7 to 356 all out in the 1981 Headingley Test?

49. Who took the very first wicket in the 2004–05 South Africa v England series?

50. Which England cricket captain also played in a FA Cup Final for Southampton and was asked to become King of Albania?

1. Which country became the ninth Test Match playing nation?

2. Which one of the following players was not fined 50% of his match fee in 2004 for an incident: Brian Lara, Rahul Dravid, Shoaib Akhtar or Glenn McGrath?

3. Which Indian cricketer completed 106 consecutive Test Match appearances?

4. Which Pakistan batsman still holds the record for the highest Test score made away from his home nation?

5. Lala Amarnath was the only bowler to have Sir Donald Bradman out in what way?

6. Can you name two of the three Australian batsman who scored more than 500 runs in the 1989 Ashes test series?

7. Who has taken 87 Test wickets at the Galle cricket ground in just 11 Test Matches?

8. Australia beat India in the 2004 series. It was the first time the Australians had triumphed in India for 15, 25 or 35 years?

9. Who led Sri Lanka to triumph at the 1996 World Cup?

10. Who played his last Test Match at the age of 50 years and 320 days old?

11. Did Michael Slater, Matthew Hayden, Brendan Julian or Shane Warne have himself tattooed with the number 356 when he was, in fact, the 357th player to have played for Australia (he was eventually given 356th status)?

12. Who was the first Zimbabwean to take 100 Test wickets?

13. Manoj Prabhakar took the wicket of which English batsman after he had batted for 633 minutes and made a triple-century?

14. Which left-handed England batsman used to bowl right arm medium pace and made 114 in his debut Test in 1993?

15. Which West Indian paceman had 269 of his 405 Test victims caught and one out, hit wicket?

16. Who is the leading run-scorer in One Day Internationals with over 13,000 runs?

17. Which South African bowler was the leading wicket-taker in Test Matches in 2003 with 59 wickets at an average of 26.54?

18. If, in the past, you were in view of the gasometer watching a bowler charge in from the Vauxhall End, at which ground would you be?

19. Which football team does former England spinner Phil Tufnell support?

20. Which Sri Lankan has scored over 9,000 One Day International runs, yet as a bowler conceded over 9,000 runs in over 330 One Day International matches?

21. Which player captained his side to a record 11 World Cup games, all of which were victories?

22. Which West Indian fast bowler was nicknamed, 'Whispering Death'?

23. Which Australian fast bowler's first Test Match wicket was his New Zealand cousin, John Reid?

24. Which English batsman became the first in 107 years to make a century in both his debut home Test Match and his debut away Test Match?

25. Which Australian off-spinner was replaced in the Australian side by Shane Warne making his Test debut?

26. At which World Cup did Australia blast 359, at the time their highest One Day International total?

27. Which England spinner took a wicket with his first ball in Test cricket in 1991?

28. In September 2003, the Multan Cricket Stadium in Pakistan became the 37th, 65th, 88th or 149th ground to host a One Day International match?

29. Who captained England in their first three-match One Day International series against Australia in 1972?

30. Which West Indies wicketkeeper played in 81 Test Matches and was never on the losing side in a Test series?

31. How many World Cups have Australia won?

32. 'Patsy' Hendren played an innings of 132 in a 1934 Test Match at the age of 45, but for which team did he play?

33. Which Test Match nation has lost 21 consecutive Tests in a row?

34. In 1946, a new rule came in allowing the fielding side in Test Matches to claim a new ball every 40 overs, every 55 overs, every 75 overs or every 90 overs?

35. How many Olympic Games have featured cricket as a medal sport?

36. Which team has drawn 301 Test Matches, far more than any other nation?

37. Which spinner took only 58 Test Matches to pass 300 Test wickets?

38. Against whom did Anil Kumble record the figures of 10 for 74 in 1999?

39. Which team has been involved in all the tied Test Matches throughout history?

40. Who was the Man of the Match in the 1999 World Cup Final?

41. Who took five wickets for just one run as Australia fell from 105-4 to all out in the 1981 Ashes Test at Edgbaston?

42. Which of the following took the most Test Matches to reach 100 Test wickets: Phil Tufnell, Ashley Giles, Carl Hooper or Heath Streak?

43. Who memorably performed a somersault after making the catch that dismissed Australia's Rod Marsh to regain the Ashes for England in 1977?

44. In which year was Bangladesh accorded Test status?

45. In 1992, Aqib Javed of Pakistan became the first player to: score 200 in a One Day International; be given out obstructing the field; be suspended by the ICC under their code of conduct?

46. Vanburn Holder is now a cricket umpire, but he played 40 Test Matches for which side?

47. Which country's first home Test was held at the Gymkhana Ground, the venue's only ever Test Match?

48. Who has played the most Test Matches for New Zealand, and is also their leading run-scorer?

49. Arthur Mailey once took 9 for 121 in a Test Match but who did he play for?

50. Who became the first player to score 3,000 runs and take 300 wickets in Test cricket?

1. Who did Australia beat in the World Cup 2003 final?

2. South African bowler Makhaya Ntini's first wicket in first-class cricket was Alec Stewart, Stephen Fleming or Mark Waugh?

3. Who went out in an Australia v England Test Match with a bat made of aluminium?

4. Who replaced Mike Brearley as England captain on the tour of New Zealand in 1977–78 when Brearley broke his forearm?

5. Was 1873, 1877, 1883 or 1887 the date of the very first Test Match?

6. Which wicketkeeper was the quickest in terms of matches to reach 200 Test Match dismissals?

7. Who was the only England cricketer to score more than 1,000 Test runs in 2003?

8. Which Pakistan fast bowler became Glenn McGrath's 400th Test Match victim?

9. Canada appeared at the World Cup in 2003. When was their only other World Cup appearance?

10. For how long was Graham Gooch banned from playing Test cricket after going on a rebel tour to South Africa?

11. Was Jack Hobbs, Ian Botham, Bob Willis or Len Sutcliffe, the only English entry in Wisden's five Cricketers of the Century?

12. Who was the 1999 World Cup Player of the Tournament with a batting average of 140.5 and 17 wickets?

13. Which West Indian fast bowler was nicknamed, 'Big Bird'?

14. Whose debut Test Match against India ended with unpromising figures of 150-1?

15. Who was the last fast bowler to captain England?

16. Who captained Pakistan for 34 matches in the 1980s and early 1990s, a record only beaten by Imran Khan?

17. Was Talha Jubair's debut against the West Indies notable as: the best debut with the ball; the most expensive bowling spell; the youngest player in World Cup history?

18. Which Australian bowler made an astonishing debut taking eight wickets in each innings?

19. Was the SCG, MCG or Perth Test Match ground rebuilt for an Olympic games?

20. Which English batsman died while batting in The Gambia in 1989?

21. In terms of the number of innings, who was the fastest to reach 1,000 One Day International runs: Sachin Tendulkar, Viv Richards, Adam Gilchrist or Andrew Flintoff?

22. Who captained India to win the First Test v Pakistan in 2004: Sourav Ganguly, Rahul Dravid or Sachin Tendulkar?

23. Which two sides together only managed 91 runs in a 1979 World Cup match?

24. Who has captained the West Indies in the most Test Matches: Brian Lara, Viv Richards or Clive Lloyd?

25. Which South African took five catches in a One Day International match against the West Indies?

26. Which British cricket broadcaster commentated on Tests from 1948 until 1980?

27. Which England player has been out for a duck the most times in Test Matches?

28. Up to October 2004, how many of Bangladesh's 32 Test Matches have ended in draws?

29. Who twice captained his country in spells of 26 consecutive Test Matches?

30. There have been only three dismissals due to 'Hit the ball twice' in Test cricket: true or false?

31. Who instructed his brother to bowl an underarm ball in a Test Match in 1981?

32. Steve Waugh managed to break into the Australian Test side in 1986. In which year did his brother follow him?

33. Which Indian batsman was first known as, 'the little master' and scored 34 Test centuries?

34. Which bowler with more than 200 Test wickets has the lowest average?

35. Which cricketer scored a fifty in 11 consecutive Test Matches?

36. Which Pakistan pace bowler took two hat tricks in two matches at Sharjah separated by seven months?

37. Which famous batsman in 2000 became Glenn McGrath's 300th test victim?

38. Which Australian bowler was Wisden's Cricketer of the Year in 1998?

39. Against which team was Sri Lanka's debut Test Match?

40. Which New Zealand cricketer took five catches in an innings against Zimbabwe in the 1997–98 season?

41. Which one player was present in the opposing team when Brian Lara scored both his 375 and his 400?

42. Was Sarfraz Nawaz, Wasim Akram or Imran Khan the third Pakistan player to score 1,000 Test runs and take 100 Test wickets?

43. In what year was the six-ball over first introduced in England: 1873, 1892, 1900 or 1924?

44. Who finished the World Cup 2003 tournament with a batting average of 163.00, the best of the tournament?

45. What is the highest ever Test score posted by Pakistan in a Test Match: 565, 647 or 708?

46. Which batsman scored 29 centuries and was knighted in 1949?

47. Which Australian batsman has an average of over 100 in Test Matches at Lord's, and an average of 268 at the Queens Park Oval?

48. Which two Australian bowlers took 58 wickets between them in the 1974–75 Ashes series?

49. Which country does not have representation in the 2004 Elite Panel of Umpires: South Africa, New Zealand or India?

50. Who has captained Australia in six Ashes Test series, more than any other captain?

1. After which umpire is the clock at the back of Headingley's West Stand named?

2. In the 2003–04 Test series against the West Indies, which batsman scored a century in each of the four matches?

3. Who scored the first ever triple-century by an Indian in a Test Match: Sunil Gavaskar, Virender Sehwag, Sourav Ganguly or Vinod Kambli?

4. Who in 1995 became the first English cricketer to take a Test Match hat trick of wickets for 38 years?

5. Which West Indian paceman's 376 Test wickets included the dismissal of Graham Gooch 16 times?

6. Who was the last person to score 1,000 first-class runs in England before the end of May 2004?

7. Was it Wavell Hinds, Chris Gayle or Jermaine Lawson who took a wicket with his first ball in One Day Internationals?

8. Who has the highest batting average for England averaging 60.72 in 54 Test Matches?

9. Which former England batsman has made four One Day International centuries yet each time found himself on the losing side?

10. One team has been involved in all the Test Matches that lasted for at least seven days. Can you name the team?

11. Who has taken more catches in Test Match cricket: Ian Botham, Stephen Fleming or Brian Lara?

12. Which wicketkeeper, with over 320 dismissals has the most in One Day International matches?

13. Who was the first non-white player to play for the Zimbabwean Test cricket team?

14. What was the name of the delivery for which Muttiah Muralitharan came under official scrutiny in 2003 and 2004?

15. Richie Benaud announced his World XI of the 20th Century in 2004. Which Indian was picked to open the batting with Jack Hobbs?

16. Against which Test nation did Zimbabwe record their highest ever score in 2001 of 563-9 declared?

17. Kapil Dev saved India having to follow on against England in 1990 by hitting which spinner for four successive sixes?

18. Which West Indian scored an innings of 192 not out versus India in his second Test Match?

19. For which English county did Australians, Ian Harvey and Darren Lehmann play in 2003?

20. How many Test wickets did English opening batsman, Geoffrey Boycott take: none, three or seven?

21. Which umpire officiated in both the Test Match where Brian Lara scored 375 and the Test Match in which he scored 400?

22. Which umpire has officiated in over 80 Test Matches, his first being in 1985?

23. Who is the only Sri Lankan outfielder to take seven catches in a single Test Match?

24. Which captain of England was wounded in World War I and had the poet, Lord Alfred Tennyson as his grandfather?

25. Which batsman played 48 tests for Australia before dying at the age of 37?

26. Who was Geoff Boycott's first opening partner in Test cricket: John Edrich, Fred Titmus or Brian Close?

27. Aravinda de Silva scored 1,220 runs in Test Matches in 1997. How many centuries did this include?

28. Can you name the one Australian Test wicketkeeper whose surname began with the letter, Z?

29. Who was the last England player to score a double-hundred in an Ashes Test Match?

30. In December 2003, which Test side saw three of their top four batsmen make 44 in the same innings against the West Indies?

31. Who took 16 English wickets in a 1998 Test Match at the Oval?

32. In the 1982–83 season, a One Day International match between New Zealand and Sri Lanka saw how many bowlers used in total?

33. Which Indian spinner became only the second bowler to take all the wickets in a Test Match innings?

34. How many tours of England did Donald Bradman make with the Australian side?

35. Which world-renowned batsman became Yorkshire's first overseas player in 1992?

36. Which Pakistan bowler took 29 wickets in a three-match Test series against New Zealand?

37. As of October 2004, who is the only cricketer still playing in county cricket whose Test batting average for England is 0.00?

38. Which West Indian fast bowler took 16 wickets in the 1976 Oval Test, nine of which saw him hit the stumps?

39. Who, in 1964, became the first ever bowler to take 300 Test wickets?

40. Who, at the age of 21 years and 75 days, was the youngest batsman to score a century in the World Cup?

41. Who was appointed the successor to Nasser Hussein as England Test Cricket captain?

42. Did David Houghton, Heath Streak or Andy Blignaut score Zimbabwe's first ever century in a Test Match?

43. Whose autobiography was entitled, *Dazzler*?

44. Allen Hill was the first ever man to: take a Test Match wicket; a Test Match catch; both?

45. India's Kiran More holds the record for the most stumpings in a Test innings. How many?

46. Which Australian seam bowler took 41 wickets in the 1989 Test series against England?

47. Which cricketer was the fastest to reach 1,000 One Day International runs: Andrew Flintoff; Michael Atherton; Marcus Trescothick or Graham Gooch?

48. Which England batsman was twice given out LBW by umpire Shakoor Rana in his debut Test Match?

49. Who, in the 1930 Ashes Test series, recorded an average of 139 which included no not outs?

50. Which Australian state side were England playing when two England cricketers buzzed the ground in Tiger Moth aircraft?

1. Who beat Australia in a 1993 Test Match by just one run?

2. Which West Indian batsman had a batting average of 104.15 at Sabina Park in some 18 Test Match innings?

3. Against which side did Clive Lloyd captain the West Indies for the first time in 1972?

4. Which England bowler took the most Test Match wickets: Dean Headley, Alan Mullally or Craig White?

5. Only two players, one from Pakistan and one from Sri Lanka, have made a One Day International century batting at number 7. Can you name either of them?

6. Which bowler was the fastest to 300, 400 and 500 Test wickets in terms of Test Matches played?

7. Against which county did Brian Lara score the highest ever first-class innings of 501?

8. Only five fast bowlers have made it to a century of Test Matches. Can you name the one Indian bowler to do so?

9. Which English county side was captained by Shane Warne in 2003?

10. Which member of the 1966 England World Cup winning football team played first-class cricket for Essex?

11. Can you name the Zimbabwean fast bowler who protested against his country's government by wearing a black armband during the 2003 World Cup?

12. Who has scored an amazing eight double-hundreds in Ashes Test Matches?

13. Which Australian player was banned for five One Day International matches in 2003?

14. Which England cricketer has captained his country more times than any other?

15. An exploding bomb near the hotel of which side two hours before the start of a 2002 Test Match forced its abandonment?

16. Who was the first batsman to score 10,000 Test runs?

17. Which West Indies fast bowler made his debut against Pakistan in 1977 taking seven wickets in that test and then recording 8-29 in the first innings of his second test?

18. How many World Cups have there been up to and including the 2003 competition?

19. Which former England captain turned out as a substitute fielder in a county cricket match in 2003 at the age of 49?

20. New Zealander, Shane Bond took 6 for 23 in the last World Cup but against which side?

21. Which Test Match playing side did Zimbabwe reduce to 17 for 5 in a 1983 World Cup match?

22. Can you name two of the three Australian umpires on the ten-strong Elite Panel of Umpires for 2004?

23. Has Martin Crowe, Jeff Crowe, Nathan Astle or Chris Cairns hit the most Test hundreds for New Zealand?

24. Who played 28 Test Matches taking 117 wickets, but was eclipsed by the batting of his younger brother and by his son who has taken 349 Test wickets?

25. Against which side did Ian Botham take 8-33 in a 1978 Test Match at Lord's?

26. Is the largest Test venue in the West Indies the Queen's Park Oval, Sabina Park or the Kensington Oval?

27. Which great West Indian batsman played in 51 Test Matches, hitting 3,860 runs, taking 69 wickets and tragically dying at the age of 42?

28. Who is the leading Test wicket-taker at the Oval ground in London?

29. Which fast bowler was hit on the head by Fanie de Villiers only to respond by bowling South Africa out with a career best 9-57?

30. Which nation holds the longest unbeaten run in Test cricket?

31. Bert 'Dainty' Ironmonger was: New Zealand's, Australia's or South Africa's oldest ever Test cricketer?

32. Was Sir Donald Bradman dismissed for a duck in his last Test Match innings by Harold Larwood, Jim Laker, Eric Hollies or Hedley Verity?

33. Against which side did Glenn McGrath record his 450th Test wicket?

34. Is Viv Richards from Antigua, St Lucia, Jamaica or Barbados?

35. Which person has umpired the most Tests?

36. Which young wicketkeeper became the captain of Zimbabwe in 2004?

37. Gilbert Jessop was a legendary fast scorer. In his first-class career he made 53 centuries. Was his average time taken to reach a century: 72, 90, 104 or 115 minutes?

38. Which Test Match batsman scored 8,231 runs and took one wicket in a total of 36 balls bowled in his Test career?

39. In which match in the four-match series between India and Australia did Sachin Tendulkar return?

40. Who scored a record 329 for Pakistan against New Zealand in a 2002 Test Match?

41. Which team holds the record for the most Test Match series in a row undertaken without defeat: England, West Indies or Australia?

42. Which side has the lowest ever total in a One Day International match out of Australia, England and Bangladesh?

43. Which side has scored the highest fourth innings total to win a Test Match?

44. In which Australian state would you find the Gabba ground?

45. Which Test umpire in 2003 surprised players in a match between Surrey and Derbyshire Second XIs, by stopping play with the score at 501 for 0 in order to photograph the scoreboard?

46. Where would you find the Kensington Oval in the West Indies?

47. Who was the wicketkeeper in Richie Benaud's World XI of the 20th Century?

48. Which side of the wicket would you find a cover point fielder: off or leg?

49. In 1999, the Riverside Stadium hosted its first full One Day International in the World Cup. Pakistan was one of the teams. Can you name the other?

50. What was the name of the son of Hanif Mohammad who played his first Test in 1983?

1. Which famous English batsman has a Test bowling career of one wicket for 165 runs?

2. Which country saw the youngest ever World Cup player debut for them in the 2002–03 competition?

3. How many sets of twins have played Test cricket?

4. Which young South African batsman made 222 not out in his debut Test Match?

5. Which side became the seventh Test Match playing nation in 1952?

6. In 2003, who scored 242 in his first innings but 0 in his second innings as his side lost to India by four wickets?

7. At which ground has Steve Waugh played more Test innings than any other?

8. Which team has been losing finalists three times and semi-finalists twice in cricket's World Cup?

9. Can you name two of the three New Zealanders who have scored over 5,000 Test runs?

10. Which cricket ground staged a Test Match first: Sydney Cricket Ground or Edgbaston?

11. Which country suffered defeat when Jim Laker took 19 wickets in a 1956 Test Match?

12. Namibia's Rudi Van Vuuren played in the 2003 World Cup and previously in a World Cup in a completely different sport. Can you name that sport?

13. Who holds the record for the highest Test innings made by a player of 45 or over?

14. In which year did Kerry Packer sign up 51 Test cricketers for his World Series?

15. Which batsman, nicknamed, Olly, weighed in at around 18 stone, and scored centuries for England before a car crash caused him to partially lose his eyesight?

16. Which South African Test cricketer of the 1960s was renowned as a magnificent fielder and was one of the first to practise by aiming at a single stump?

17. Which Sri Lankan cricketer has the initials before his surname of, W P U J C?

18. Which current international umpire has stood in more One Day Internationals than any other?

19. Which Indian batsman did John Snow knock over when he was attempting a run, with Snow dropped for a match as punishment?

20. Which English bowler took 6-33 in the Riverside's first ever Test Match: Jimmy Anderson, Steve Harmison or Richard Johnson?

21. Who is the youngest ever person to captain a Test side when he led out his team versus Sri Lanka in 2004?

22. Which batsman has scored more Test hundreds than any other current player?

23. Hugh Tayfield bowled 137 balls in a Test Match without conceding a run. What nationality was he?

24. In which country has one city had four different Test Match grounds?

25. Which English ground saw an epic confrontation in 1998 between English batsman, Michael Atherton and South African pace bowler, Allan Donald?

26. Which former England fast bowler averaged just 6.05 runs with the bat in his 58 Test Match innings?

27. Who is the only Pakistani fast bowler to play in 100 Test Matches?

28. In 1938, simulated broadcasts of Test Matches were made by Australia that featured a pencil tapped to make the sound of the bat hitting the ball: true or false?

29. Who umpired in all three of the first World Cup cricket finals?

30. Who on his One Day International batting debut, scored a one-day century against Sri Lanka in just 37 balls?

31. Against which side did Glenn McGrath start his 100th Test Match?

32. Which English cricketer holds the record for the longest Test Match playing career of 30 years and 315 days?

33. Which batsman has an astonishing Test Match batting average of 192.00 at the Headingley cricket ground?

34. Which one of the following English cricketers has not made 50 or more in eight consecutive Tests: Ken Barrington, Andrew Flintoff, Alec Stewart or Graham Gooch?

35. Ian Botham was not in Richie Benaud's World XI of the 20th Century: true or false?

36. Which English ground was the only one in 2004 to host a Test Match that started at 11am?

37. Which English cricketer presided as captain over 12 matches that resulted in four draws and eight defeats?

38. Who was out hit wicket versus India in his 165th Test Match: Glenn McGrath, Javed Miandad or Steve Waugh?

39. Which team has played the most Test Matches: New Zealand, Pakistan or South Africa?

40. Which Indian left-handed batsman of the 1990s had a Test batting average of 54.20 in his 17 matches?

41. Which fast bowler captained England from 1982 until 1984?

42. Who captained Australia for 93 Test Matches?

43. Who has won more One Day International Man of the Match awards for Australia than any other player?

44. Who averaged 63.3 in the 2002–03 Ashes series, the highest on either side?

45. For which country did Dipak Patel play 37 Test Matches?

46. Two players who were or became England captains have been out, handled the ball, in Test cricket. Can you name them?

47. Three English bowlers have taken 15 wickets in one Test Match, all three playing against the same nation. Which nation was it?

48. Which English Test cricketer has a painting hanging in Australia's Sir Donald Bradman museum?

49. Which team was the first to win the World Cup Final batting last?

50. Which South African recorded an innings of 275 beating Hugh Tayfield's 274 as the record Test score at the Kingsmead, Durban ground?

1. Which English cricketer has played consecutively the most One Day International matches (over 90 in total)?

2. For which Australian state side did Ian Botham play in 1987–88?

3. In the 1983 World Cup, who came in when his side had fewer than 20 on the board and went on to score 175 including six sixes?

4. Which Zimbabwean cricketer has made four One Day International centuries, yet each time found himself on the losing side?

5. How many matches against the West Indies had Ian Botham previously played before he ended up on the winning side?

6. Who, at just over 18 years of age, is New Zealand's youngest ever One Day International player?

7. Did Brian McKechnie, Jeff Crowe, Richard Hadlee or Bev Congden face the infamous

underarm ball bowled by Australia's Trevor Chappell in a Test Match?

8. Which Australian wicketkeeper was dubbed 'iron gloves' in his early career but had the last laugh, taking over 350 Test dismissals?

9. Which side became the eighth Test Match playing nation?

10. Which Australian batsman with the middle name Laurence has already hit 20 centuries in just 55 tests and has twice scored centuries in both innings of a Test Match?

11. Who was the first black player to represent England in Test cricket?

12. Which England captain became Dennis Lillee's 100th victim in Test cricket?

13. Against which side did Hanif Mohammed hit an innings of 337 in January 1958?

14. Which Pakistan batsman played for Lahore, Habib Bank and Essex and in the 1991 season scored a total of 1,972 runs?

15. Which England batsman didn't score a run in his first Test Match in 1975?

16. Who finished their career with more Test Match dismissals: Alan Knott; Jeff Dujon; Jack Russell?

17. Who was the first country to contest a Test Match against England at the Riverside Stadium?

18. Australia's Colin McCool played 14 Test Matches for his country: true or false?

19. Which Pakistan wicketkeeper has taken the most Test dismissals, finishing his career with 201 catches and 27 stumpings?

20. Nolan Clarke played in a World Cup at the age of 47, making him the oldest ever World Cup player but for which side did he play?

21. Can you name either of the England batsmen who put on a record 176 run stand for the second wicket at the 1975 World Cup?

22. Who scored 8,558 Test runs for his country when batting in the first innings and 2,369 runs in second innings?

23. Garry Sobers is famous for hitting six sixes in one first-class over, but which Indian Test cricketer was the next to achieve this feat?

24. In the Fourth Test of the 1989 Ashes series, which England player scored more runs in an innings than all of his teammates put together: Ian Botham; Graham Gooch; David Gower; Jack Russell or Robin Smith?

25. Which former Australian captain, despite suffering a bout of malaria, scored 123 not out in an Ashes Test Match at Melbourne: Warwick Armstrong, Richie Benaud, Allan Border or Mark Taylor?

26. Which Pakistan batsman has a highest Test Match score of 188 not out, but has an even higher One Day International score of 194, the highest ever recorded?

27. Which wicketkeeper walked in the semi-final of the 2003 World Cup when playing Sri Lanka?

28. Whose Test Match captaincy record for South Africa reads: captained four times, won the toss four times and won all four matches?

29. Which New Zealand all-rounder retired in 2004 having taken 217 Test wickets and scored 3,320 runs?

30. Which Indian bowler took at least one wicket in 42 consecutive Test Match innings during the 1970s?

31. Which South African captained his country 53 times out of his 68 Tests?

32. Which England captain bowled 408 balls in Test cricket, taking two wickets with a bowling average of 151?

33. Which West Indian fast bowler had a total of 48 not out innings in his Test Match career?

34. As of October 2004, who is the only person to captain his side to more than 100 One Day International wins?

35. How many nine-day long Test Matches have occurred?

36. In 2001, Craig McMillan took a record 26 runs off one over in a Test Match off which Pakistan bowler: Waqar Younis, Younis Khan or Inzamam-ul-Haq?

37. What do all of these England players have in common concerning their debut Test Match: Keith Fletcher, Michael Atherton, Alan Knott and Len Hutton?

38. Who was Harold Larwood's bowling partner in the infamous Bodyline Test series?

39. In what year was the first World Cup held?

40. How many England players have scored over 8,000 Test runs?

41. How many players did England use as bowlers in the first innings of the 1976 Oval Test against the West Indies?

42. Which two teams contested a Test Match believed to be the first witnessed by a President of the United States?

43. Which Test captain brought himself on to bowl when England were at 887 for 7 and fell, breaking his tibia?

44. Which Test ground in England saw its first streaker in 1975?

45. Were Dominic Cork's dramatic hat trick of wickets against the West Indies in 1995, all LBWs, all caught or all bowled?

46. Which Test side's longest unbeaten streak ran for 26 Tests between 1968 and 1971?

47. Which Indian spinner's highest Test Match innings was 206 made in an innings against Australia where Sachin Tendulkar made 148?

48. Which player has scored the most first-class runs in his career?

49. Can you name either of the bowlers who dismissed Graham Gooch for a duck in his debut Test Match?

50. Clayton Lambert has played for two different countries in official One Day International matches. Can you name the countries?

1. Can you name either of the two English bowlers who have bowled more than 21,000 balls in Test Match cricket?

2. Did Allan Border, Clive Lloyd, Viv Richards or Michael Vaughan score 1,710 runs in one calendar year?

3. Which player has played 54 One Day International matches for one national side and 55 for another?

4. Can you name two of the three West Indian players who have scored more than 8,000 Test Match runs?

5. Which side recorded the lowest ever innings total in a Test Match?

6. In the fourth Ashes Test in 1981, for how many runs did Botham take five wickets in a spell of 28 balls?

7. Did Ricky Ponting, Michael Clarke or Adam Gilchrist become the 17th Australian to score a century in his debut Test Match?

8. Which New Zealander survived 77 balls without scoring for the longest duck in Test cricket?

9. How many times in Test Matches were batsmen out caught Rodney Marsh, bowled by Dennis Lillee?

10. How many tied Test Matches have there been?

11. The Test cricket stadium in Lahore, Pakistan is named after which foreign leader?

12. Who were the last two brothers to play for England in a One Day International or Test Match?

13. Who averaged 45.7 in the 2003 World Cup to be England's highest averaging batsman?

14. Which team made 509 runs in a single day of a 2002 Test Match?

15. Which England Test batsman started his career in 1932 with Norfolk, played for Middlesex and returned to Norfolk for whom he played up until 1972?

16. If the 'Black Caps' were playing the 'Proteas', which two Test-playing sides would you be watching in action?

17. Which captain of Middlesex made his England test debut in 2004?

18. Which team in 2004 were set just 108 to win but were bowled out for 93, the third lowest target in a fourth innings which a team has lost?

19. Wisden's five Cricketers of the Century contained two West Indians. Can you name them?

20. Who played 356 One Day International matches, taking 502 wickets?

21. At what ground did Shane Warne bowl Mike Gatting with what became known as, 'the ball of the century'?

22. How many Chappell brothers played cricket for Australia?

23. Was Tony Greig, Mike Brearley or Ray Illingworth captain of England in the Test Match where Dennis Lillee used an aluminium bat?

24. A 1984 India v Pakistan Test Match was abandoned due to the assassination of which Indian Prime Minister?

25. Against which Test side did Bangladesh's Mohammad Ashraful make 158 in a 2004 Test Match?

26. Which batsman has Glenn McGrath dismissed 19 times in Test Matches?

27. Which England batsman played for Arsenal football club in the 1950 FA Cup Final?

28. Yousuf Youhana compiled a very fast Test Match fifty against South Africa. Did it take 23, 27 or 31 balls?

29. Did Bill Edrich, Mike Gatting or Jack Hobbs once score 1,000 first-class runs, all at Lord's cricket ground, before the end of May?

30. Who went 119 Test Match innings without being out for a duck?

31. Who finished the four-match series versus Australia in 2004 with an extraordinary batting average of 123.80?

32. Which side has the lowest ever total in a One Day International match out of Namibia, Sri Lanka and Pakistan?

33. Which England fast bowler, often bowled in tandem with Fred Trueman, took 100 or more first-class wickets in a season 13 times throughout his career?

34. Which one of the following English umpires did not play Test cricket for his country: Peter Willey, Jeremy Lloyds or Mark Benson?

35. Was David Boon, David Gower or David Houghton the leading run-scorer at the 1983 World Cup?

36. In 1996, Sanath Jayasuriya hit an incredible 134 in 48 balls, which included 11 fours and 5, 8 or 11 sixes?

37. Which batsman and captain of his country was nicknamed, 'the master blaster'?

38. Which all-rounder with the middle name, Terence, became the first to score a century and take ten wickets in a Test Match?

39. In which year did Sri Lanka play their first Test Match?

40. Peter Kirsten played 12 matches for South Africa in the 1990s. Who was his half-brother who has become South Africa's leading run-scorer?

41. Javagal Sriniath took six wickets for 21 runs in the 1996–97 Test Match against which side?

42. Who started the 1972 season with back trouble, but went on to take 31 English Test wickets?

43. In the winter of 2001–02, which side whitewashed Zimbabwe and the West Indies in a Test Match series?

44. Which former England cricketer's autobiography was entitled, *Opening Up*?

45. Which country was the first to broadcast radio commentary of cricket matches?

46. Which batsman first played 24 Test Matches for Australia in the 1980s before switching to South Africa?

47. Against which side did West Indies score 276 for the first wicket in the first innings, yet lost the Test Match?

48. Can you name either of the Pakistan players who have captained their side in more than 100 One Day International matches?

49. Who won the first cricket World Cup?

50. Which bowler with 330 Test Match wickets was nicknamed, 'White Lightning'?

1. Against which English county did Australia score 721 runs in a single day while touring?

2. Which England bowler took the most Test Match wickets: Peter Lever; Richard Ellison or Pat Pocock?

3. How many of Mike Proctor's seven Test Matches ended in a win for South Africa?

4. Can you name the former Zimbabwean batsman-wicketkeeper who protested against his country's government by wearing a black armband during the 2003 World Cup?

5. Which young West Indian all-rounder made his Test debut at Lords in 2004 and went on to score 220 runs and take 16 wickets in the four-match series against England?

6. Canadian, John Davison scored a lightning-fast 67-ball century in the 2003 World Cup against which side?

7. Which West Indian fast bowler has the middle names, Alexei McNamara?

8. Who averaged over 100 for Australia in the 2003–04 India v Australia Test series?

9. In which city would you find the Kingsmead Test Cricket ground?

10. Which former England Test captain took a rebel team to South Africa in 1989?

11. Wayne Larkins' return to Test Cricket in 1989–90 was after a gap of six, nine or 11 years?

12. Which West Indian had won more Test Match Man of the Match awards than any other prior to November 2004?

13. Against which side did New Zealand's Chris Cairns record match figures of 10/100 in a Test Match in the 1999–2000 season?

14. Gary Kirsten hit a score of 188 not out in the 1996 World Cup, but was it against Canada, Bangladesh, the United Arab Emirates or Kenya?

15. Against which team did England reach 17 for 3 before the entire Test Match was abandoned after just 10.1 overs?

16. Which England captain was fined £2,000 in 1994 for ball tampering?

17. Which former England batsman was nicknamed Arkle and turned out for Suffolk at the age of 49?

18. Which Sri Lankan player has batted in every position from opener to number 10 in One Day Internationals?

19. Which West Indian cricket captain donated blood to help save the life of India's captain, Nari Contractor, after he had been hit in the head by a ball?

20. Which team has only won 21 of its 182 Tests away from home?

21. Douglas Jardine, Colin Cowdrey and Robin Jackman all played for England, but in which Test Match playing country were the three born?

22. Who holds the record for the most consecutive Test Match appearances by a West Indian: Desmond Haynes; Garry Sobers or Brian Lara?

23. Which Pakistan spin bowler helped bowl Sussex to the English county championship in 2003 taking 103 wickets?

24. Whose Test debut series saw him score two centuries and have a batting average of 75.57 only for it to be his last Test series?

25. Sir Garfield Sobers made 18, 26 or 32 Test Match centuries?

26. In which year did 50 overs per side become the standard format for One Day International matches?

27. Who is the only Pakistan bowler to take 40 wickets in a Test Match series?

28. Who captained Australia to their World Cup 2003 win?

29. Which West Indian fast bowler knocked out four of Ian Botham's teeth in a domestic one day match?

30. Which Australian batsman was dismissed five times in the 1990s in Tests against England?

31. Who bowled 1,279 maidens in Test cricket, far more than any other English bowler?

32. Alec Bedser is the leading Test wicket-taker at two English grounds. Can you name either of the grounds?

33. At which Australian ground is the Boxing Day Test traditionally held?

34. Which English batsman scored three consecutive centuries against Australia in the 1985–86 Ashes series?

35. Which Indian cricketer was named the ICC's Cricketer of the Year in 2004?

36. Which ground became England's seventh Test Match venue: Old Trafford; Bramall Lane; Wembley or The Oval?

37. Who scored 340 in an innings against India and 253 in an innings versus Pakistan?

38. Against which side did Jeremy Coney score more of his Test runs than any other?

39. Who has made the most runs in an Ashes series in England for England?

40. Which England cricketer was born in Hong Kong: Phil Tufnell; Dermot Reeve or Derek Randall?

41. In what year was the cricketer's reference bible, *The Wisden Cricketers' Almanack*, first published: 1864, 1892, 1907 or 1919?

42. South Africa's Centurion Park was first used as a Test Match cricket venue in 1936, 1948, 1966 or 1995?

43. Who topped the batting averages at the 1996 World Cup with 120.50 from six matches?

44. Against which country did Dipak Patel take 23 of his 75 Test Match wickets?

45. In the 1977–78 season, which side scored 445 runs in the fourth innings of a Test Match yet still lost?

46. Which Zimbabwean holds the record for the highest ever One Day International innings on debut?

47. In 1989, who became the youngest Test Match player to score a fifty?

48. Which South African's innings of 275 in the 1999–2000 season took over 14½ hours to complete?

49. How many Test wickets did Don Bradman take?

50. Which bowler has taken 76 Test wickets at Eden Park, more than double the number of any other bowler?

1. Which wicketkeeper holds the record for the most dismissals and the fifth most dismissals in a Test Series, together totalling 54 dismissals, all caught?

2. Which England opener was the first cricketer to score a 99 in One Day International matches?

3. Sarfraz Nawaz played for which Test Match nation?

4. Which Indian batsman was known by the nicknames, 'The Noob' and 'Tiger'?

5. What is the northernmost Test Match cricket ground in the world?

6. Who is the only New Zealand outfielder to take seven catches in a single Test Match?

7. Which Australian bowler took 82 Test wickets at the Melbourne Cricket Ground, almost twice as many as the second leading wicket-taker at that ground?

8. Who, at four days short of his 45th birthday became England's oldest ever One Day International cricketer?

9. Was the last time England won the Ashes: 1987, 1991, 1994 or 1996?

10. In one Test Match in 2004, three bowlers, all of whose surnames begin with the letter K, took all the wickets in an innings. Can you name two of them?

11. Who is the holder of the highest not out score in a Test Match: Garry Sobers, Brian Lara or Viv Richards?

12. Which Indian batsman scored 13 Test centuries against the West Indies?

13. Who has scored the most Test centuries against Australia?

14. Which player has scored 12 double hundreds in Test Matches, more than any other player?

15. Name the two African nations who made it through to the Super Six stage of the 2003 World Cup?

16. Bert Sutcliffe played 42 Test Matches for which country?

17. Against which team in 1991 did New Zealand record their highest Test innings of 671-4 declared and their highest individual score of 299?

18. Which Australian opening batsman was out LBW as often as he was out caught in his Test career, and in 2004 was Bangladesh's coach?

19. Who took 6 for 19 in a 2000 One Day International match against England to record the best One Day International bowling figures by a Zimbabwean?

20. Who has captained India in more One Day Internationals than any other skipper?

21. Which cricketer featured on the first cricket-themed British stamp released by the Post Office in 1973?

22. Who was the third man to take 200 wickets and score 2,000 runs in Tests?

23. Who led New Zealand in 34 consecutive Tests retiring after a 1965 series against England?

24. In which month of 2004, did Brian Lara score 400 not out against England?

25. Which batsman has scored the most Test runs in a calendar year?

26. Which member of the 2004 New Zealand side to tour England was born in Australia: Scott Styris; Nathan Astle or Mark Richardson?

27. How many tests did it take Ian Botham to complete 100 wickets and 1,000 runs?

28. Which Indian bowler scored a duck with the bat in each innings of the Fourth Test v Australia in 2004?

29. Who partnered Peter May when the pair put on 411 for the fourth wicket against the West Indies in 1957?

30. Mugs misprinted with the nickname, King of Spain instead of King of Spin featured which England bowler?

31. Which English county had a long association with Sir Richard Hadlee?

32. Which England cricketer was awarded the MBE in 1998, the OBE in 2003 and bowled 3.2 overs in Test Match cricket?

33. Which Sri Lankan batsman has scored 9,284 One Day International runs including 64 scores of 50 or more?

34. In 1966, England's number 10 and number 11 batsmen managed to forge a record 128-run partnership for the last wicket. Can you name either player?

35. Who was the first West Indian wicketkeeper to take nine catches in a Test Match?

36. In the 1999 World Cup, which country staged its first ever One Day International match, between the West Indies and Bangladesh?

37. Which bowler with over 400 Test wickets never took a Zimbabwean or South African wicket?

38. Who made 226 in his first innings at the Gabba, which has remained the highest score for over 75 years?

39. Which famous all-rounder was David Gower's only wicket in Test Matches?

40. Which England player scored his maiden Test century against New Zealand in 2002?

41. Can you name the one New Zealand wicketkeeper to take more than 200 dismissals in Tests?

42. Who has stood as an umpire in over 160 One Day International matches, more than any other official?

43. Whose Test Match batting average was 59 against Australia, 86 against Sri Lanka and 22.14 against West Indies?

44. Who has taken the most wickets in total in Ashes Test Matches?

45. Which Sri Lankan bowler took 8 for 19 in a One Day International against Zimbabwe?

46. For which team did Austin Codrington take five wickets in the 2003 World Cup?

47. What number One Day International shirt does Andrew Symonds wear for Australia?

48. Who took more wicketkeeping dismissals for England in Test Matches: Bob Taylor; Jack Russell or Paul Downton?

49. Which Australian fast bowler's best Test figures were 8-97 against England?

50. Whose batting average was almost 23 runs higher when he captained England compared to the 75 times he played for England as non-captain?

1. Which Australian opener, nicknamed 'the happy hooker' became the first Australian to be given out for handling the ball in a Test Match?

2. Which South American country is the only one on the continent to feature a Test Match venue?

3. Who is best known by his last two names which are preceded by the four names, Warnakulasuriya Patabendige Ushantha Joseph?

4. In the mid-1980s, did Derek Pringle, Wasim Akram or Paul Reiffel become the youngest bowler to take ten wickets in a Test Match?

5. Whose scores of 333 and 123 in two innings of a Test against India are a record aggregate in a single match?

6. Which member of the West Indies fast bowling quartet captained by Clive Lloyd later trained and worked as an airline pilot?

7. Which team did England beat twice to reach the final of the 1992 World Cup?

8. Was a monsoon, pitch vandalism or an earthquake responsible for the Second Test between India and Australia in 2004 ending in a draw?

9. How many runs did Steve Waugh score in his very last Test Match innings: 0, 7, 48, 80 or 107?

10. How many runs did Don Bradman need to score in his last Test innings to end his career with a batting average of exactly 100?

11. Can you name two of the three Englishmen who have scored 22 Test centuries, the most by an English cricketer?

12. Sidath Wettimuny was the first cricketer to score a Test century, but for which country?

13. 1,764 runs were scored in a 1968–69 season Test Match between which two sides?

14. At the 1999 World Cup, name two of the three competing nations who had not played a Test Match?

15. Who, in 1953, became the first professional cricketer to receive a knighthood?

16. Which cricketer played just ten Tests for the West Indies during the 1980s, but was on the winning side in every match?

17. Who is New Zealand's leading wicket-taker with 431 Test scalps?

18. Which England cricketer topped Yorkshire's county championship batting averages in 2003 with an average over 65?

19. Two players have captained India a record number of times (47 Test Matches). Who are they from the following list: Sourav Ganguly; Mohammad Azharuddin; Rahul Dravid; Sachin Tendulkar; Sunil Gavaskar?

20. Who made more appearances for the West Indies: Courtney Walsh; Viv Richards; Gordon Greenidge?

21. What is the most balls bowled in a single Test Match: 2,918, 3,602, 4,298 or 5,447?

22. Which former World War II fighter pilot was nicknamed, 'Nugget' and scored 2,958 runs and took 170 Test wickets for Australia?

23. Which Indian player has hit more One Day International sixes than any other: Sunil Gavaskar; Sachin Tendulkar or Sourav Ganguly?

24. Who beat Namibia by an incredible 256 runs in a One Day International match in the 2002–03 season?

25. Did Stephen Fleming, Jacob Oram or Craig McMillan make 126 not out in the first innings of the Australia v New Zealand Test Series in 2004?

26. Who is the only West Indian to have bowled over 30,000 deliveries in Test cricket?

27. How many times did Ian Botham take five wickets in an innings and score a century in the same Test Match?

28. Which two young English batsmen made a partnership of 291 at Lord's in 2004, the third highest made at that ground?

29. Who has scored the fastest century in One Day Internationals?

30. Which English slow left-arm bowler took 14 wickets in a single day against Australia in 1934 and died in a POW hospital in Italy in 1943?

31. Which New Zealand wicketkeeper hit his first century in October 2004 against Bangladesh?

32. Which bowler has taken the most Test wickets in a calendar year?

33. Which two Australians averaged more than 60 for the 2002–03 Ashes series?

34. Which Australian batsman once recorded Test bowling figures of 7-46?

35. Can you name both of the teams who competed in cricket's first-ever tied test in 1960–61?

36. Was Sri Lanka's first Test Match staged at Colombo, Newlands, the MCG or Lord's?

37. Which Australian cricketer has scored the most Test Match runs without ever getting a century?

38. How many players have scored centuries in their country's first ever Test Match?

39. Was Imran Khan, Zaheer Khan or Mohsin Khan the only Pakistan player to be given out for handling the ball in Test cricket?

40. Which former Australian test cricketer became Australia's best-selling author in 1990 with the books: *How to Hypnotise Chooks*; *How to Tame Lions* and *How to Kiss a Crocodile*?

41. Which English cricketer has made the most Test Match appearances?

42. Against which nation did Matthew Hayden make his career best 380 in 2003?

43. Which team, in their very first One Day International, beat Australia?

44. Which all-rounder took 383 wickets, 120 catches and scored 5,200 runs in their Test career?

45. There have been only two dismissals due to being Timed Out in Test cricket: true or false?

46. Which fast bowler did not score a run in 28 consecutive second innings of Test Matches?

47. Which English batsman smashed the stumps after being given out when on 139, but is now on the ICC's panel of Elite Referees?

48. How many Ashes series did Sir Donald Bradman captain Australia?

49. Who was the first bowler to take 500 Test wickets?

50. Which West Indian in 1972 became the first ever cricketer to score centuries in both innings of his debut Test?

1. In which city would you find the Jade Stadium Test Match cricket ground previously known as Lancaster Park?

2. Tom Garrett appeared in the very first Test Match and remained: the youngest; the oldest; the most successful bowler in Test Matches for 53 years?

3. Which West Indian bowler became the first to take a hat trick at the Gabba in 1988?

4. In which World Cup did Kenya memorably beat the West Indies by 73 runs?

5. Who was refused entry into Guyana causing one of the 1979–80 Test Matches between England and the West Indies to be cancelled?

6. Name Ricky Ponting's partner in their record 2003 World Cup final partnership of 234?

7. Who, in 1994 became the first overseas umpire in the modern era to stand in a Test Match in England?

8. Who, in the 1930 Ashes series, recorded scores of 131, 254, 334 and 234?

9. Who has taken seven Test wickets in an innings for the fewest number of runs: Ian Botham; Michael Holding; Stephen Harmison; Dennis Lillee?

10. Who, in a 2002 Test Match, came in to bat against New Zealand with the score on 57 and was out when the score had progressed to 643?

11. Which Chappell brother had a highest score of only 27 against England?

12. Which former West Indian captain, with the middle name Hubert, is now one of the ICC's Elite Panel of Match Referees?

13. Which English all-rounder's debut series in 1995 saw him score 197 Test runs and pick up 26 wickets?

14. Was Brian Close, David Gower, Andrew Flintoff or James Foster the youngest player to play a Test Match for England?

15. What is the name of the Indian wicketkeeper who made 198 Test dismissals and also took a Test wicket via his bowling?

16. Which side has played the third most Test Matches in total?

17. Which side notched up an incredible 509 runs in a single day's play in a 2002 Test Match?

18. In which country were there eight balls in an over between 1936 and 1979?

19. Which fast bowler finished his Test Match career in 1994 having taken 434 wickets and having scored 5,248 runs?

20. Which bowler took an astounding 8-24 to bowl out Pakistan for 72 in December, 2004?

21. Who has captained his team in more World Cup games than any other captain?

22. Which is the only team in entire Test Match history to have won more Test Matches away from home than they have lost?

23. Only one host nation has won the World Cup. Who was it?

24. Which England batsman accompanied David Gower when he buzzed team mates in a light aircraft during the 1991 Ashes tour?

25. Who was the captain of Australia during the Bodyline series of 1932?

26. If you were watching an anecdotes show called 'Beef and Lamb' which two English cricketers would you be viewing?

27. Which wicketkeeper scored 94 in his Test Match debut against Sri Lanka in 1988?

28. How many matches were there in the first two World Cups: 15, 27, 39 or 48?

29. Which West Indian made a score of 214 in his debut Test Match in 1971 versus New Zealand?

30. Which side recorded the highest all-out Test Match score of 849 against the West Indies?

31. What was Australian cricketer Bill O'Reilly's nickname: Rocket; Tiger; Stumper?

32. Who holds the record for the most dismissals by a wicketkeeper in a Test Match?

33. How many of the 70 youngest players to play a One Day International were New Zealanders?

34. For which Test side does Dave Mohammad ply his spin bowling?

35. Which Pakistan player was only the second cricketer in the world to reach 10,000 One Day International runs?

36. Which former England Test batsman has scored over 36,000 first-class runs and is still playing for an English county?

37. Which West Indian fast bowler captained South African side Natal in 1993–94?

38. Who was the quickest Sri Lankan to reach 1,000 One Day International runs: Sanath Jayasuriya; Roy Dias; Aravinda de Silva or Hashan Tillakaratne?

39. In 1882, who took 7-44 in the second innings to win the Test Match from which the Ashes were named: WG Grace, George Lohmann or Fred Spofforth?

40. Mohammad Sharif debuted in an official One Day International when he was not even 16 years of age. From what country did he come?

41. Which New Zealander rewrote the record books with a double-hundred against England completed in just 153 balls?

42. How many consecutive Test Matches did Australia go in a row without a draw in the period 1999 to 2001?

43. Which Indian batsman, in 1969, was the first Test cricketer to score a duck in his debut Test innings and then score a century in the second innings?

44. In 2003, Sri Lankan Ajith Cooray was banned from cricket for how many years for assaulting an umpire?

45. Prior to the 2005 Ashes series, which Australian had taken 132 English Test wickets?

46. Which member of the West Indian 2004 team to tour England was born in Los Angeles, USA: Ridley Jacobs; Tino Best; Marlon Samuels?

47. Which English county did Shane Warne captain in 2004?

48. Chris Cairns' career Test Match batting average was 33.53, but against which Test side was his average 74?

49. At which Test Match ground did Jim Laker take 19 wickets in a match?

50. Did the West Indies go for 11, 15, 21 or 29 consecutive Test Match series without defeat in the 1970s and 1980s?

1. In which year did India win their first Test Match series in Pakistan?

2. Sir Len Hutton is the only Test Match player to be out as a batsman in which way?

3. Which fast bowler's highest score at the 2003 World Cup was 43 yet, due to not outs, finished the tournament with a batting average of 72.00?

4. In 2002, only one England player was fined a percentage of his match fee by the ICC. Who was it?

5. Which Australian player notched a hundred before lunch in a 1975 World Cup match against Sri Lanka?

6. Has Jeff Dujon, Ridley Jacobs or Rashid Latif taken more Test Match dismissals as wicketkeeper?

7. Who, on his way to a Test innings of 334, actually scored a century in each of the day's three sessions of play?

8. Which team were asked to follow-on by their opponents yet managed to win the Test Match by an incredible 171 runs, the same number that they scored in their first innings?

9. How many of the 70 youngest players to play a One Day International were English?

10. St George's Park hosted the first Test Match to be played outside of Australia or England. In which country is it found?

11. England's greatest batsman of his era ran out Don Bradman in Bradman's first Ashes Test Match in 1928. Who was he?

12. Which ground first held a Test Match: Old Trafford or Lord's?

13. Who once took seven West Indian wickets, including Viv Richards, in an innings at the Sydney Cricket Ground?

14. Who was the first batsman to score a five in Test cricket by hitting the fielder's helmet?

15. Seven Australian cricketers made centuries in six Test Matches in 1993. The Waugh brothers were two. Can you name three of the other five?

16. Which Pakistan legend batted an incredible 970 minutes, over 16 hours, when making 337 in a Test Match?

17. International umpire Aleem Dar comes from; Pakistan; India; Bangladesh; Sri Lanka?

18. Who captained South Africa in Test Matches and One Day Internationals during the period 1994 to 2000?

19. Since 1982, can you name three of the five England players who have captained their side in two Ashes Test series?

20. Which England batsman recorded the remarkable feat of scoring 3,816 first-class and Test Match runs in the 1947 season?

21. Against which side in 1998 did Inzamam-ul-Haq bowl his, so far, only balls (9 in total) in Test Match cricket?

22. If you were watching Test Cricket at the Supersport Park, in which country would you be?

23. Which captain of Australia was nicknamed, 'the Big Ship' and weighed approximately 20 stone?

24. Which side won the Women's World Cup in 2000?

25. West Indian, David Holford and his cousin shared an unbeaten 273 run stand against England in the 1966 Lord's Test. Who was the cousin?

26. Who is the leading Test wicket-taker at all of Sri Lanka's current Test cricket venues?

27. Which Australian batsman scored over 11,000 Test runs?

28. Who scored 1,503 Test runs in 2003, beating Brian Lara as the heaviest scorer in that year?

29. Why was the 1998 Test Match at the Iqbal Stadium, Pakistan cancelled?

30. Who hit Sri Lanka's first half-century in Test cricket?

31. How many One Day International wickets did Mike Gatting take: one, three, six or ten?

32. Which Pakistan batsman has scored 18 hundreds and has an average of over 49 in Test cricket?

33. Which Australian batsman scored 32 Test centuries, but only one Test double century?

34. Which captain of New South Wales became the first batsman to score a hundred before lunch in a Test Match?

35. Which Indian spinner's bowling figures read 12-8-6-1 against East Africa in the 1975 World Cup?

36. Which country's leading Test wicket-taker took more than double the country's second placed player on the list?

37. In the 1956 'Laker Test' what was the name of the English bowler who got the only wicket not to fall to Jim Laker?

38. Which Englishman took a world record 4,024 first-class wickets in a career lasting 30 years?

39. Who is the only player in world cricket to, as of November 2004, average more than one six per One Day International innings?

40. Harold Larwood played professional football for Notts County as well as bowling for England: true or false?

41. What name is given to the England cricket supporters who follow their team around the globe?

42. Which two Australian brothers shared a Test cricket stand of 464?

43. Which England batsman's grandfather played Dr Who on television?

44. In a 1988 Test Match, Pakistan notched up the most extras in an innings. Within five, can you guess the number?

45. Whose autobiography, *Leading From The Front*, was banned from sale from all county cricket grounds and was given as one of the reasons for his removal as England Test captain?

46. Which West Indian all-rounder was born with an extra finger on each hand?

47. Which non-wicketkeeper has taken the most catches in total in Test Matches?

48. Which English bowler in 1978 took two wickets with consecutive balls, bowled a no-ball and then took two more wickets with consecutive balls?

49. At what position did Steve Waugh score over 6,000 runs, more than in any other position?

50. Can you name two of the three players who have scored Test centuries against all the Test playing nations including Bangladesh and Zimbabwe?

1. Which country will host the 2005 Women's World Cup?

2. Australian batting legend, Victor Trumper, once scored a rapid 50 for Paddington versus Waverley off how many scoring balls?

3. Who produced a devastating spell of pace bowling to take six wickets for 24 runs to dismiss England for 46 in a 1994 Test Match?

4. In which year was overarm bowling legalized: 1864, 1888, 1896 or 1907?

5. Was WG Grace, Fred Spofforth, Johnny Briggs or Harold Larwood the first ever bowler to take 100 Test wickets?

6. Who has won the most World Cup games as captain: Steve Waugh; Clive Lloyd; Ricky Ponting; Kapil Dev?

7. Billy Midwinter became the first cricketer to play both for and against which cricketing nation?

8. Which highly successful Australian batsman and captain had to wait 42 innings before scoring his maiden Test century?

9. The first World Cup final ended at 8.43pm, but did it start at 11am, 1.30pm or 2.45pm?

10. Which team finished third in the 2003 World Cup Super Six table and played India in the semi-final of the competition?

11. Which former England bowler's father and grandfather both played for the West Indies?

12. Which Test Match captain only lost four of the 27 matches he captained and went on to have a long career in the media?

13. Which Pakistan bowler passed 200 Test wickets in 1995 at the tender age of 24?

14. Which West Indian fast bowler formed a record 106 partnership for the 10th wicket with Viv Richards in a 1984 One Day International against England?

15. Three cricketers have been named the BBC Sports Personality of the Year. Ian Botham was the last one in 1981. Can you name either of the two others?

16. Which spin bowler has taken five wickets in a Test Match innings 44 times?

17. Which former Australian captain's Test batting average was 116.0 when batting at number four, but only 30.0 when batting at number five?

18. Who is the only England player to have scored four double-hundreds against Australia in Ashes Test Matches?

19. Which Hollywood actor owns his own cricket ground and has former New Zealand captain, Martin Crowe as a first cousin?

20. Which batting legend scored a Test century against England in just 56 balls?

21. Who captained the formidable South African side who whitewashed Australia in the 1969–70 Test series?

22. Which Australian batsman scored over 1,100 runs on the 1993 tour of England, but was not selected for the Test Matches?

23. Habidul Bashar scored over 800 runs in 2003, but for which Test nation does he play?

24. How many Test Matches have South Africa played on neutral grounds?

25. Can you name the three great West Indian batsmen of the late 1940s onwards, known together as the Three Ws?

26. Who was dropped after his first two Tests for England in 1975 and did not play again until 1979 when he went on to appear a further 116 times?

27. Which legendary batsman made only 18 and one in his first Test Match and was dropped as a result?

28. Can you name either team that has played at the Bundaberg Rum Stadium in Cairns against Australia in a Test Match?

29. How many years elapsed before India recorded their first ever Test Match victory?

30. Which English cricket captain has a perfect winning record, the first achieved since Lord Hawke in the 1890s?

31. At which English ground did Sachin Tendulkar score his first Test century for India?

32. Was the very first Test Match won by: 3, 29, 45, 102 or 177 runs?

33. Which New Zealander has captained his side in more One Day Internationals than any other?

34. Which two English Test Match grounds both staged their first Test in 1899?

35. Which Western Australian, nicknamed Garth, was, in his era, the youngest cricketer to reach both 100 and 200 wickets in Test cricket?

36. Which two England players from the 1970s and 1980s jointly hold the record for the most consecutive appearances in Test Matches?

37. Who captained the West Indies when they played South Africa in their first 1992 Test Match?

38. What is the most number of tests in a row that Australia have lost?

39. Which national captain confessed to match fixing in 2000?

40. Who is the leading run-scorer in One Day International matches with over 12,000 runs?

41. Who was Bangladesh's opponents in their very first Test Match?

42. Which Australian batsman made a world record 153 consecutive appearances in Test Matches?

43. Who was the first ever cricketer to be knighted for services to cricket while still playing Test cricket?

44. Which Test cricket venue is the only sports ground in New Zealand declared a heritage site?

45. Was Zimbabwe's first Test Match held in Mumbai, Harare or Johannesburg?

46. How many balls were there in an over in the first ever Test Match?

47. Which Indian fast bowler reached 100 Test wickets when he was still only 21 years of age?

48. Whose previous high score against Bangladesh was 18 before he smashed a double century in December 2004?

49. Who became a Test Match playing nation first: India, New Zealand or Pakistan?

50. Who became the first Australian in 100 years to make his first ever first-class century in a Test Match?

1. Who played his last Test Match at Trent Bridge at the age of 50 years, 320 days?

2. Which England bowler took 236 Test wickets and went on to become an England selector for 23 years?

3. Which English cricketer also played football for Queens Park Rangers, Manchester City and Brentford?

4. In the 1994–95 Ashes series, who took the first hat trick in an Ashes series for over 90 years?

5. Who has scored 775 Test runs in just two innings at the Recreation Ground, Antigua?

6. Which famous all-rounder's middle name was St Aubrun: Richard Hadlee; Kapil Dev; Garry Sobers; Ian Botham?

7. Who in 2001, faced 452 balls against Australia hitting 44 fours in his innings?

8. How old was the youngest ever One Day International player, Pakistan's Hasan Raza?

9. Who recorded a record eight sixes in a World Cup innings in 2003?

10. Who captained his country to 193 One Day International matches, more than any other skipper?

11. In which country would you find the Kingsmead cricket ground?

12. Which West Indian batting legend was sacked as coach of Bangladesh just prior to their surprise defeat of Pakistan in the 1999 World Cup?

13. Who made 65 consecutive Test appearances for England between 1971 and 1977?

14. Which team plummeted to 47 all out in a 2004 Test Match versus England?

15. Who took most Test Match wickets out of the following: Chris Lewis; Mike Hendrick; Frank Tyson?

16. Which New Zealand venue has hosted more Test Matches than any other: Basin Reserve; Eden Park or Westpac Park?

17. What was the name of the twins who were born in 1918 and played for Surrey throughout their careers?

18. How many times have English bowlers taken six wickets in a One Day International match?

19. Of the 10 leading England Test run-scorers who has the most not out innings?

20. George Headley was famous for scoring four Test centuries before what age?

21. Who ordered his brother to bowl an unhittable delivery in the last ball of a 1981 One Day International?

22. Who came out of retirement in his forties to lead Australia to a series win over India, hitting two centuries in the process?

23. What is the name of the Johannesburg Test Match venue that features the Unity Stand, the Taverner's Pavilion and the Memorial Stand?

24. Who holds the record for the most catches made in Test Matches by a West Indian fielder other than a wicketkeeper?

25. Which English batsman has the nickname, 'Banger' because of his fondness for sausages?

26. Alok Kapali took a hat trick of Test Match wickets in 2003, but for which nation?

27. Which New Zealander was the 1992 World Cup's leading run-scorer with 456 runs?

28. How many Test Match wickets did Dennis Lillee take in 1981: 42, 57, 63 or 85?

29. In the summer of 2004, England had eight batsman who made Test centuries. Can you name five of them?

30. Which Australian captain scored a total of 426 runs in a Test against Pakistan including a triple century?

31. Can you name both teams unable to play a Test Match due to fog?

32. John Traicos was born in Egypt but played Test cricket for which two nations?

33. Was Vinoo Mankad, Javed Miandad or Kapil Dev the first Indian batsman to make a century against Australia?

34. Which bowler took 33 wickets in just a three-match Test Series against Australia in the mid-1980s?

35. Before the 1994–95 tour, in which season had Australia last beaten the West Indies: 1975–76; 1982–83 or 1988–89?

36. Against which side did Kiran More take the record for the most stumpings in an innings?

37. Which Sri Lankan made a rapid half century in a One Day International match against Pakistan in just 17 balls?

38. Which Indian batsman was the first ever cricketer to be given out in a Test Match by the third umpire?

39. Which country is the only one not to play Test cricket but has hosted Test Matches?

40. Which Sri Lankan bowler took a hat trick of Test wickets with his first three balls of a match against Zimbabwe?

41. Which batsman and which bowler retired from Test Match cricket at the end of the same series as their team mate, Rodney Marsh?

42. Which side scored 411 in the final innings of a Test Match yet lost by 193 runs to Australia?

43. Up to October, 2004, have 7, 13, 15 or 29 batsmen scored a century in their very last Test Match?

44. Which Australian batsman holds the record for the most catches in Test cricket with a total of 181 in 128 matches?

45. Which spinner has taken 59 Test wickets at the National Stadium in Pakistan, more than any other bowler?

46. Which West Indian batsman hit Matthew Hoggard for six consecutive fours in a 2004 Test Match?

47. Which Pakistan player once scored 257 not out when coming into bat at number eight?

48. Which West Indian wicketkeeper made seven dismissals in a Test Match innings versus Australia in 2001–02?

49. Which England bowler won one Test Match cap as has his son, Ryan, the latter in 2001?

50. Who succeeded Garry Sobers as captain of the West Indies: Rohan Kanhai, Alvin Kallicharran or Clive Lloyd?

1. Which wicketkeeper played in more Test Matches than any other?

2. Which slow left-arm bowler took over 100 wickets in a season for Yorkshire nine times and died of wounds sustained during World War II?

3. Whose record did Ian Botham pass in 1986 to become the leading Test wicket-taker?

4. Who finished the World Cup 2003 tournament with a batting average of 117, the second best of the tournament: Sachin Tendulkar; Gary Kirsten, Andy Bichel; Scott Styris?

5. Four players have scored a century in their 100th Test Match. Can you name two of them?

6. India's Chetan Sharma was the first player to manage which feat at a World Cup?

7. Against which side did Trevor Chappell infamously bowl an underarm delivery in 1981?

8. The Rawalpindi Cricket Stadium first hosted a Test Match in 1936, 1953, 1976 or 1993?

9. Who is England's leading Test Match run-scorer of all time?

10. What is the lowest score ever recorded in a Test Match: 19, 26, 38 or 43?

11. The 1989–90 series between Pakistan and India was the first time: a white ball had been used; neutral umpires stood; a stumpcam was used; a wicketkeeper took 12 catches?

12. Which Pakistan legend is the only player to have taken hat tricks of wickets twice in Test cricket and One Day International matches?

13. Which Indian cricketer was sent home in disgrace from England in 1936 only to captain India 10 years later?

14. Which Indian spinner bowled 12 overs for six runs in the 1975 World Cup?

15. At which ground have England won more Ashes Test Matches than at any other?

16. How old was Sachin Tendulkar when he was appointed captain of India in 1997?

17. Which team featured three brothers who all played together against New Zealand in the 1969–70 season?

18. After which two players is the Test series between India and Australia named?

19. What is wicketkeeper 'Jack' Russell's real first name?

20. Whose autobiography was entitled, *Menace*?

21. Which West Indian bowler became only the fifth bowler in history to take 400 Test wickets?

22. Which England fast bowler pulled out of the 2004 tour of Zimbabwe citing personal reasons?

23. Which team has twice recorded its lowest ever total for an innings of 30 runs?

24. Of the top five highest ever Test Match innings, how many were made by West Indian batsmen?

25. At which Test Match ground is Jimmy Anderson the leading wicket-taker?

26. Who made a fifty when Ian Botham performed heroics in the second innings of the 1981 Ashes test at Headingley?

27. Whose one Test Match as captain of England in 1999 ended in a draw against New Zealand?

28. Against which side did England score 1,121 runs in a single Test Match, the record aggregate?

29. Which foreign side has lost only one of their last 26 Test Matches at Lord's?

30. Which Australian fast bowler took 212 Test wickets, including dismissing Richie Richardson nine times?

31. Which England all-rounder became the 100th player in Test cricket to take 100 Test wickets?

32. Which Australian captain averaged 115 against Zimbabwe in Test Matches?

33. Can you name either of the joint leading wicket-takers in the 2002–03 Ashes series?

34. Which Indian batsman scored 10,122 Test runs at an average of 51.12?

35. Who scored a record 365 in a Test innings at the tender age of 21?

36. Which South African all-rounder has batted in every position from opener to number 10 in One Day Internationals?

37. Which team won the first two World Cups?

38. Which West Indian opener made a century on his debut in One Day Internationals in 1976?

39. Which bowler took 23 wickets at the World Cup and had the best average of his team?

40. Who is the only England batsman to have scored over 2,000 Test runs at Lord's?

41. Which team has twice notched a total of 70 in One Day International innings, their lowest ever score?

42. Did India win their first Test series in England in 1958, 1967, 1971 or 1982?

43. Who conceded 710 runs in a four Test Match series in 2003–04: Brett Lee; Ashley Giles; Anil Kumble; Fidel Edwards?

44. Which England cricket captain and, later, chairman of the selectors, stood at an election against Labour MP, and later, Prime Minister, James Callaghan?

45. Which England batsman smashed the stumps out of the ground after being given out in the one-off Bicentenary Test against Australia in Sydney?

46. Can you name two of the three surnames of the pairs of brothers who have played for Zimbabwe?

47. The Beausejour Stadium became the West Indies' newest Test venue in 2003, but is it found on Antigua, Jamaica, St Lucia or Grenada?

48. Which country saw the father score that nation's first Test century only for his son to score that nation's 100th Test century some 40 years later?

49. Who holds the record for most ducks in Test cricket with 43 instances of being out scoring nought?

50. Thami Tsolekile replaced who in the South African side for the winter 2004 Test series against India?

1. Which much-loved umpire officiated in 66 Tests and retired in 1996?

2. During a dispute between England and Australia in the 1909 Headingley Ashes Test, which English batsman stepped away from his wicket to let himself be bowled?

3. Which team has hit more One Day International centuries than any other?

4. In the 2003–04 series versus England, which Sri Lankan bowler took 26 wickets and had a batting average higher than Marcus Trescothick, Andrew Flintoff, Mark Butcher and Nasser Hussein?

5. Which South African all-rounder was only able to play seven Test Matches scoring 226 runs before his country was excluded from Test cricket?

6. Excepting Zimbabwe and Bangladesh, which two countries are the only ones not to have a Test bowler with over 400 Test wickets?

7. Who bowled 55.3 overs conceding just 51 runs in the very first Test Match?

8. What is the highest not out score made in a Test Match: 333, 365, 380 or 400?

9. Which two brothers were born in Durban, South Africa but played Test cricket for England?

10. Which opening batsman has been out for 13 runs in Test Matches more than any other: Michael Atherton; Geoffrey Boycott; Mark Waugh; Gordon Greenidge?

11. What was the name of the media magnate behind World Series Cricket in the late 1970s?

12. In which Australian state would you find the MCG cricket ground?

13. Which team scored 952 against India in a Test Match?

14. How many Test Matches have been won by a side asked to follow-on: one, three, seven or fifteen?

15. Who was the oldest ever West Indian to play in a World Cup: Garry Sobers, Lance Gibbs or Courtney Walsh?

16. Can you name either of the teams who tied a One Day International match in the 2003 World Cup?

17. Which South African city held the famous 'Timeless Test' in 1939?

18. How old was New Zealander Daniel Vettori when he took his 100th Test wicket?

19. Who in 2002–03 was the first West Indian bowler to take a hat trick in Test Matches since Courtney Walsh in 1988–89?

20. Name either of the Sri Lankan batsmen who produced a record 576 run second wicket partnership against India in 1997–98?

21. Which West Indian legend holds the record for the highest Test innings made by a player of 20 years of age or under?

22. Which English cricketer is the only non-South African to have recorded one of the five highest Test scores at the Centurion Park ground?

23. Who is the only wicketkeeper to take six dismissals in a One Day International match more than twice?

24. Was the lowest total to win a One Day International: 87, 99, 118 or 131?

25. Which West Indian batsman recorded a score of 148 in his first One Day International match?

26. Who played 203 Test Match innings as an opening batsman?

27. Who was the only Australian not dismissed by Sarfraz Nawaz in the second innings of the First Test in 1979?

28. Richie Benaud announced his World XI of the 20th Century in 2004. Can you name the one Pakistan player in his team?

29. Which South African wicketkeeper has made more Test Match dismissals than any other?

30. Jimmy Sinclair was the first player to both score a century and take five wickets in an innings in a Test Match. What nationality was he?

31. Which former Australian captain's middle name is Rodger?

32. Which England all-rounder, as a 15 year old, scored 234 not out in a 20-over game?

33. What was the surname of the five brothers, four of whom played Test cricket for Pakistan?

34. Who in 1982 reached a double century in 220 balls, at the time the fastest double-hundred in Test Match history?

35. Which batsman has twice hit 30 runs off of a single over in a One Day International match?

36. Which player has been captain in the most Tests?

37. Did Viv Richards, Lawrence Rowe or Alvin Kallicharran score 302 out of 598 made against England in a 1974 Test Match?

38. Which West Indian cricketer took 5-41 and scored 119 in a One Day International match versus New Zealand?

39. Who batted for 277 minutes, making 29 not out, in order to save a Test Match against South Africa in the mid-1990s?

40. Which was the only nation Mike Proctor played Test Match cricket against?

41. In the Fourth Test between India and Australia in 2004, who scored ducks in both innings?

42. The South African team which faced Australia in Adelaide in 1998 contained how many players who had or would go on to make Test centuries?

43. Against which side did England play their first match of their 2004 tour to Zimbabwe?

44. Is Sydney Barnes, Devon Malcolm or Darren Gough the only English bowler to have taken more than 15 wickets in a Test against South Africa?

45. Which son of a former England captain bowled Phil Simmons with his very first ball in Test Cricket?

46. Who, in 2003, walked off at the Oval, out LBW for 38 in his last Test Match?

47. Which side played only five Test Matches in 2003, the least of any nation?

48. Which English bowler took 20 wickets in back-to-back Tests in the Caribbean in 1998?

49. Which Indian player averages approximately 51 in Tests with seven hundreds and a highest score of 309?

50. Who has played more Test Match innings as a number 11 batsman than any other player?

1. Which Australian captain struck a Test Match hundred in just 78 minutes in the 1954–55 season?

2. And who was the hundred against?

3. Which England batsman secured an incredibly lucrative advertising deal in the 1940s believed to be worth £1000 a year?

4. Which current England cricketer played chess as a schoolboy for Lancashire?

5. Which was the only Test playing side not to draw a Test Match in 2003?

6. Which Indian cricketer scored 164 against South Africa in November 2004 to take his tally of runs in the year past 1,000?

7. In which decade did the BBC's Test Match Special broadcasts begin?

8. Who was made captain of an England team for the first time for England's second match against Namibia in November, 2004?

9. Which current Test captain was just 22 years of age when he was given the captaincy?

10. Can you name either of the players who took part in England's record One Day International partnership of 226 in 2004?

11. Which Australian averaged over 65 runs in 31 One Day International matches in 2003?

12. Who bowled a ball at the 2003 World Cup measured at 100.2mph?

13. In which century was the first Lord's cricket ground established in London by Thomas Lord?

14. Nick Knight used to hold the English record for the most Test Matches played without ever playing Australia. His record was 17. Who holds the record with over 40?

15. In which country would you be watching Test cricket if you were present at the Bellerive Oval?

16. And does Sachin Tendulkar, Michael Slater or Sherwin Campbell hold the record for the highest score there?

17. Who has taken 75 Test wickets at the Bulawayo ground, over 40 more than the next highest wicket-taker?

18. Who made scores of 277 and 259 in back-to-back Tests against England in 2003?

19. Can you name both players who forged India's record partnership in a One Day International match of 331?

20. Which New Zealander played 58 Tests for his country, but never played against Australia?

21. Which Indian cricketer made 16 Test half-centuries but never a hundred: Virender Sehwag, Chetan Chauhan or Aakash Chopra?

22. Which current Test cricketer has taken over 145 Test Match catches?

23. Can you name any of the batsmen Matthew Hoggard dismissed when he took a Test hat trick in 2004?

24. Which English bowler took 252 Test wickets of which 102 were bowled?

25. Who, as of November 2004, had bowled more than 5,400 overs in Test cricket, the most of any bowler?

26. Which Australian bowler has conceded the most runs in 10 overs in One Day International matches?

27. Who has taken four wickets in a One Day International innings 27 times?

28. Who took the most Test wickets in 2003: Makhaya Ntini, Steve Harmison, Glenn McGrath or Anil Kumble?

29. Which Australian pace bowler when on tour in England bowled a tennis ball against Leicestershire and an apple against Sussex?

30. Which West Indian fast bowler has played 38 Test Matches but never a Test against England: Corey Collymore, Ian Bishop or Merv Dillon?

31. Name the most successful Test bowler/wicketkeeper partnerships in terms of wickets taken caught behind by the wicketkeeper.

32. Who bowled 3,031 overs in One Day Internationals, the most of any bowler?

33. In 1998, who took 80 Test wickets, more than any other bowler?

34. Who has taken the most Test wickets in matches between India and Pakistan?

35. Which West Indian bowler has taken the most English Test wickets: Courtney Walsh; Malcolm Marshall; Curtly Ambrose?

36. R.G. Nadkarni bowled 32 overs in the 1963–64 Test Match in Madras versus England. How many runs did those 32 overs go for?

37. Who was the first New Zealand captain to win a Test Match, the first, fourth or eighth?

38. How many English Test Match captains have there been: 35, 48, 56 or 75?

39. Who captained South Africa only once, losing a 1998 Test Match?

40. Which Australian ground has hosted more Test Matches than any other?

41. Which player has won a record 50 Man of the Match awards in One Day Internationals?

42. Prior to the Winter tour to Zimbabwe and South Africa, which England player had won more One Day International Man of the Match awards than any other?

43. Hamilton Masakadza made a Test century against West Indies in 2001. How old was he at the time?

44. Which player has scored over 9,800 One Day International runs and taken over 250 One Day International wickets?

45. Who was the Indian captain who appealed to the umpire to reverse his decision to give England's Bob Taylor out in the Golden Jubilee Test at Bombay?

46. In which country would you find the Defence Housing Authority Stadium which has hosted one Test Match?

47. Who is the leading English wicket-taker against West Indies in Test Matches?

48. Who was England's leading Test wicket-taker in 1998: Darren Gough; Dean Headley; or Angus Fraser?

49. Gubby Allen once bowled an over in a 1934 Test Match that contained three wides and how many no balls?

50. Three Zimbabweans have captained their side for 20 or more Test Matches. Can you name two of them?

1. Which former footballer with Manchester United played in a Test Match for England in 1985?

2. Which Test wicketkeeper broke his nose at the age of ten, the first time he used a set of wicketkeeping gloves bought for him as a present?

3. Which two pairs of brothers have both scored centuries in both innings of a Test Match?

4. Between 1993 and 1998, one Indian cricketer played in 21 Test Matches without ever being on the losing side. Can you name him?

5. Who is the only ever Test batsman to score a not out century in both innings of a single Test Match?

6. Which West Indian player with five Test Matches completed has West Indian greats, Alvin Kallicharran and Rohan Kanhai as his uncles?

7. What was the fishy name of Yorkshire's first-choice wicketkeeper for 20 years whose Test batting average for England was 0.5 runs per innings?

8. Which Bangladesh player scored a century in his country's first ever Test Match?

9. Which legendary batsman of the turn of the 20th century is considered to have invented the leg glance shot and in 1915 lost most of the sight in his right eye?

10. What was the name of South Africa's 10th Test Match venue used in 2002 when South Africa entertained Bangladesh?

11. Whose kneecap, removed in 1955, shortly after he made 492 runs in the Test series against South Africa, was kept by the surgeon and donated to the MCC?

12. Who was knocked unconscious by a ball from Harold Larwood during the infamous Bodyline Test series between Australia and England?

13. What is the most westerly Test Match venue in the world?

14. As of October 2004, how many players with the first name, Shane, have played Test cricket?

15. Which bowler was picked for England in 1901 without ever having played first-class cricket, but went on to take 189 Test wickets in just 27 Tests?

16. Who has scored the most Test runs for England in a calendar year?

17. What was the name of the Bangladesh player who carried his bat through a Test Match versus Zimbabwe, scoring 85 out of his side's total of 168?

18. Can you name, in the correct order, the four captains used by England in a five Test series against the West Indies in 1988?

19. Who, in the 20th century, was the only Australian to have bowled two consecutive overs in a Test Match?

20. Which Indian-born player stood down from playing for England in 1929 when the opposing team, South Africa, objected to his inclusion?

21. Which leg-spinner was born in New Zealand, went to Australia on a short holiday and stayed there 66 years taking 216 Test wickets for his adopted country?

22. Who hit a record 12 sixes in a Test Match innings?

23. Which Pakistan batsman is their second leading run-scorer and has scored three times as many Test centuries as Imran Khan?

24. What was the name of the Australian batsman who was the only player to score 1,000 runs in a calendar year before World War II?

25. Which West Indian legend's son is David Murray and his grandson is Ricky Hoyte?

26. How many Test centuries did West Indies wicketkeeper Jeff Dujon make in his career?

27. Which Sri Lankan captain had the unenviable World Cup record of played 12, lost 11?

28. Which bowler claimed Sir Donald Bradman's wicket in Test Matches more times than any other?

29. England's Frank Woolley played under more Test captains than any other player. How many?

30. Australian, Ernie Toshack has the most economical five wickets figures in a Test Match innings. How many runs did he take his five wickets for?

31. Which batsman was at the non-strikers end when Geoffrey Boycott scored his 100th century, and was also there when John Edrich did the same?

32. In 1878, Australia played the first ever first-class match in the United States. What was the name of the opposition?

33. Which Australian captain bowled practice balls for around 18 minutes, keeping his Ashes opponent waiting at the crease to face his first delivery?

34. At which other sport did WG Grace represent England?

35. Who is the only Nobel Prize winner to have played first-class cricket?

36. Up to and including October 2004, what was the lowest total achieved in an official One Day International match?

37. What was the name of the Australian bowler who became the 1975 World Cup's leading wicket-taker even though he only played in two matches, the semi-final and final?

38. Which talented Australian all-rounder cricketer also played 50 games for the St Kilda Australian Rules team?

39. What was the name of the Indian Prince who on his Test Match debut against Australia scored 62 and 154 not out?

40. Which New Zealand Test batsman scored 206 against England in 1949, but also played one Rugby Union International for England against Ireland?

41. Who lost most of the sight in his right eye in a car accident, but went on to captain India in 22 of the 46 Test Matches he played?

42. What was 'Patsy' Hendren's real first name?

43. Who, as of October 2004, held the record for the most consecutive Test appearances by a Sri Lankan?

44. Which Pakistan player holds the record for the slowest century made in Test cricket, taking 557 minutes in the 1977–78 season?

45. Which New Zealand player made nought in a Test Match innings despite being in for 101 minutes?

46. Which Australian fast-medium bowler appeared in the Australian drama, Flying Doctors?

47. In which year did New Zealand win their first Test Match in England?

48. Which Indian bowler in 1997 took a wicket with his very first ball in Test cricket, but failed to ever take another?

49. Who was an English selector in 1956 when his fellow selectors persuaded him to play against Australia, aged 41?

50. What is the record number of years in a row that the Ashes has been held by one team?

Answers

Quiz 1

1. Michael Vaughan, Marcus Trescothick
2. Australia and England
3. Wasim Akram
4. Michael Clarke
5. Geoffrey Boycott (played 2, won 2)
6. New Zealand
7. George Lohmann
8. Australia
9. Malcolm Marshall
10. Sharjah CA Stadium
11. Lala Armarnath (father), Surinder Armarnath (son)
12. Greg Chappell
13. VVS Laxman
14. West Indies
15. Tiger Moth
16. Frank Worrall
17. England
18. Sussex, Surrey, Nottinghamshire
19. True
20. Over 1,700
21. Sri Lanka
22. Shane Warne
23. New Zealand
24. Number five
25. Andrew Flintoff
26. Courtney Walsh
27. New Zealand
28. Sanath Jayasuriya
29. Terry Alderman
30. Eight times
31. Zimbabwe
32. 8-43
33. Pakistan
34. Eden Park, Auckland
35. Viv Richards
36. Robin Smith
37. Jermaine Lawson
38. John Snow
39. Rudi Koertzen
40. Virender Sehwag
41. Everton Weekes
42. Bob Willis
43. Richard Hadlee
44. India
45. True
46. India
47. Stuart MacGill
48. Marvin Atapattu
49. Stephen Harmison
50. 20th

Quiz 2

1. David Gower
2. Jim Laker
3. Rahul Dravid
4. Nasser Hussein
5. England
6. Garry Sobers
7. New Zealand
8. 18
9. 1,981
10. England
11. Imran Khan
12. England
13. Rusi Surti (played for Queensland)
14. Alex Stewart
15. Michael Atherton
16. Stephen Fleming
17. Jack Russell
18. Sanath Jayasuriya
19. Durham
20. Dwight Eisenhower.
21. Sachin Tendulkar
22. Three
23. Fred Trueman
24. Kepler Wessels
25. Abdul Razzaq
26. Michael Vaughan
27. Three (Wilfred Rhodes, George Gunn, WG Grace)
28. Abdul Qadir
29. Bill Lawry, Bobby Simpson
30. Mushtaq Ahmed
31. The same
32. Chaminda Vaas
33. 49 wickets
34. Five
35. Muttiah Muralitharan
36. Sixty
37. Timed Out, obstructing the field, handling the ball, hit wicket, hit the ball twice.
38. Wasim Akram
39. Charles Bannerman
40. Graham Gooch
41. Bob Willis
42. Zaheer Abbas
43. Viv Richards
44. Mark Taylor
45. Australia
46. West Indies
47. Lord's
48. Ten times
49. Worcestershire
50. Sri Lanka

Answers

Quiz 3

1. Douglas Jardine
2. 90
3. Ramnaresh Sarwan
4. Stuart MacGill
5. 298
6. Shane Warne
7. Mushtaq Ahmed
8. Rahul Dravid
9. The Riverside, Chester-Le-Street,
10. Herschelle Gibbs, Jacques Kallis
11. 1934
12. Namibia
13. 81
14. 14 times
15. Godfrey Evans
16. Sir Donald Bradman, Shane Warne
17. Basil D'Oliviera
18. West Indies
19. Derek Underwood
20. Allan Donald
21. Andrew Hall
22. Michael Atherton
23. Sri Lanka
24. Mickey Stewart (79.50)
25. Bill Lawry (Australia), Colin Cowdrey (England)
26. Sir George ('Gubby') Allen
27. Curtly Ambrose
28. Stephen Fleming
29. Graham Hick
30. Galle International Stadium, Sri Lanka
31. Graham Thorpe
32. Out, handled the ball
33. Mark Waugh
34. Fred Trueman
35. Sunil Gavaskar
36. The World Cup
37. Alan Knott
38. Joey Benjamin
39. Dudley Nourse
40. John Wright
41. Wes Hall
42. Melbourne Cricket Ground
43. Garry Sobers
44. Craig McMillan
45. Ian Botham
46. West Indies
47. Viv Richards (1976)
48. Chris Old, Graham Dilley, Bob Willis
49. Matthew Hoggard
50. Charles Burgess (CB) Fry

Quiz 4

1. Zimbabwe
2. Glenn McGrath (he was fined 25%)
3. Sunil Gavaskar
4. Hanif Mohammed
5. Hit wicket
6. Mark Taylor, Steve Waugh, Dean Jones
7. Muttiah Muralitharan
8. 35 years
9. Arjuna Ranatunga
10. WG Grace
11. Michael Slater
12. Heath Streak
13. Graham Gooch
14. Graham Thorpe
15. Curtly Ambrose
16. Sachin Tendulkar
17. Makhaya Ntini
18. The Oval
19. Arsenal
20. Sanath Jayasuriya
21. Ricky Ponting
22. Michael Holding
23. Bruce Reid
24. Andrew Strauss
25. Peter Taylor
26. 2003 World Cup
27. Richard Illingworth
28. 149th
29. Brian Close
30. Jeff Dujon
31. Three
32. England
33. Bangladesh
34. Every 55 overs
35. One
36. England
37. Muttiah Muralitharan
38. Pakistan
39. Australia
40. Shane Warne
41. Ian Botham
42. Carl Hooper
43. Derek Randall
44. 2000
45. Suspended by the ICC under their code of conduct
46. West Indies
47. India
48. Stephen Fleming
49. Australia
50. Ian Botham

Answers

Quiz 5

1. India
2. Alec Stewart
3. Dennis Lillee
4. Geoff Boycott
5. 1877
6. Adam Gilchrist
7. Marcus Trescothick
8. Waqar Younis
9. 1979
10. Three years
11. Jack Hobbs
12. Lance Klusener
13. Joel Garner
14. Shane Warne
15. Bob Willis
16. Javed Miandad
17. The youngest player in World Cup history
18. Bob Massie
19. The MCG, Melbourne
20. Wilf Slack
21. Viv Richards (21 innings)
22. Rahul Dravid (he stood in for injured captain, Ganguly)
23. Canada and England
24. Clive Lloyd
25. Jonty Rhodes
26. John Arlott
27. Michael Atherton (20)
28. Three
29. Hansie Cronje
30. False (none)
31. Greg Chappell
32. 1992
33. Sunil Gavaskar
34. Malcolm Marshall (20.94)
35. Viv Richards
36. Wasim Akram
37. Brian Lara
38. Glenn McGrath
39. England
40. Stephen Fleming
41. Graham Thorpe
42. Sarfraz Nawaz
43. 1900
44. Andrew Symonds
45. 708
46. Donald Bradman
47. Allan Border
48. Dennis Lillee and Jeff Thomson
49. India
50. Allan Border

Quiz 6

1. Dickie Bird
2. Jacques Kallis
3. Virender Sehwag
4. Dominic Cork
5. Malcolm Marshall
6. Graeme Hick
7. Wavell Hinds
8. Herbert Sutcliffe
9. Robin Smith
10. England
11. Brian Lara
12. Adam Gilchrist
13. Henry Olonga
14. The Doosra
15. Sunil Gavaskar
16. West Indies
17. Eddie Hemmings
18. Viv Richards
19. Yorkshire
20. Seven
21. Darrell Hair
22. David Shepherd
23. Hashan Tillakaratne
24. Lionel Tennyson
25. Victor Trumper
26. Fred Titmus
27. Seven
28. Tim Zoehrer
29. Nasser Hussein (207) in 1997
30. South Africa
31. Muttiah Muralitharan
32. Sixteen
33. Anil Kumble
34. Four
35. Sachin Tendulkar
36. Waqar Younis
37. Gavin Hamilton
38. Michael Holding
39. Fred Trueman
40. Ricky Ponting
41. Michael Vaughan
42. David Houghton
43. Darren Gough
44. Both
45. Five
46. Terry Alderman
47. Michael Atherton (25 innings)
48. Mike Gatting
49. Sir Donald Bradman
50. Queensland

Answers

Quiz 7

1. West Indies
2. Garry Sobers
3. India
4. Dean Headley (60)
5. Mohammad Kaif, Hashan Tillakaratne
6. Muttiah Muralitharan
7. Durham
8. Kapil Dev
9. Hampshire
10. Geoff Hurst
11. Henry Olonga
12. Sir Donald Bradman
13. Darren Lehmann
14. Michael Atherton (54)
15. New Zealand
16. Sunil Gavaskar
17. Colin Croft
18. Eight
19. Graham Gooch
20. Australia
21. India
22. Simon Taufell, Daryl Harper, Darrell Hair
23. Martin Crowe (17 hundreds)
24. Peter Pollock
25. Pakistan
26. Queen's Park Oval
27. Frank Worrell
28. Ian Botham
29. Devon Malcolm
30. West Indies (27 matches)
31. Australia's
32. Eric Hollies
33. India
34. Antigua
35. Steve Bucknor (91 Tests by October, 2004)
36. Tatenda Taibu
37. 72 minutes
38. David Gower
39. The third match
40. Inzamam-ul-Haq
41. West Indies
42. Australia
43. West Indies
44. Queensland
45. Billy Bowden
46. Bridgetown, Barbados
47. Adam Gilchrist
48. Off
49. Scotland
50. Shoaib Mohammad

Quiz 8

1. Jack Hobbs
2. Bangladesh
3. One
4. Jacques Rudolph
5. Pakistan
6. Ricky Ponting
7. Melbourne Cricket Ground
8. England
9. Stephen Fleming, Martin Crowe, John Wright
10. Sydney Cricket Ground
11. Australia
12. Rugby Union (1999 World Cup)
13. Jack Hobbs (159)
14. 1977
15. Colin Milburn
16. Colin Bland
17. Chaminda Vaas
18. David Shepherd
19. Sunil Gavaskar
20. Richard Johnson
21. Tatenda Taibu
22. Sachin Tendulkar
23. South African
24. Sri Lanka (Columbo)
25. Trent Bridge
26. Devon Malcolm
27. Wasim Akram
28. True
29. Harold 'Dickie' Bird
30. Shahid Afridi
31. India
32. Wilfred Rhodes
33. Sir Donald Bradman
34. Alec Stewart
35. True
36. Headingley
37. Ian Botham
38. Steve Waugh
39. New Zealand
40. Vinod Kambli
41. Bob Willis
42. Allan Border
43. Mark Waugh
44. Michael Vaughan
45. New Zealand
46. Graham Gooch, Michael Vaughan
47. South Africa
48. Jack Russell
49. Sri Lanka (1996)
50. Gary Kirsten

Answers

Quiz 9

1. Marcus Trescothick
2. Queensland
3. Kapil Dev
4. Andy Flower
5. 19
6. Daniel Vettori
7. Brian McKechnie
8. Rodney Marsh
9. Sri Lanka
10. Matthew Hayden
11. Roland Butcher
12. Mike Brearley
13. West Indies
14. Salim Malik
15. Graham Gooch
16. Jeff Dujon
17. Zimbabwe
18. True.
19. Wasim Bari
20. The Netherlands
21. Dennis Amiss and Keith Fletcher
22. Steve Waugh
23. Ravi Shastri
24. Jack Russell
25. Warwick Armstrong
26. Saeed Anwar
27. Adam Gilchrist
28. Ali Bacher
29. Chris Cairns
30. Bishen Bedi
31. Hansie Cronje
32. Michael Atherton
33. Courtney Walsh
34. Allan Border
35. One
36. Younis Khan
37. They all made a duck in their debut Test Match
38. Bill Voce
39. 1975
40. Four
41. Nine
42. Pakistan, Australia
43. Sir Donald Bradman
44. Lord's
45. All LBWs
46. England
47. Ravi Shastri
48. Jack Hobbs
49. Jeff Thomson and Max Walker
50. West Indies and USA

Quiz 10

1. Ian Botham, Derek Underwood
2. Viv Richards
3. Kepler Wessels
4. Brian Lara, Viv Richards and Garry Sobers
5. New Zealand
6. One
7. Michael Clarke
8. Geoff Allott
9. 95
10. Two
11. Colonel Gadaffi
12. Adam and Ben Hollioake
13. Paul Collingwood
14. Sri Lanka
15. Bill Edrich
16. New Zealand and South Africa
17. Andrew Strauss
18. Australia
19. Sir Garfield Sobers, Sir Vivian Richards
20. Wasim Akram
21. Old Trafford
22. Three
23. Mike Brearley
24. Indira Ghandi
25. India
26. Michael Atherton
27. Denis Compton
28. 27 balls
29. Bill Edrich
30. David Gower
31. Rahul Dravid
32. Pakistan
33. Brian Statham
34. Jeremy Lloyds
35. David Gower
36. 11 sixes
37. Sir Vivian Richards
38. Ian Botham
39. 1982
40. Gary Kirsten
41. South Africa
42. Dennis Lillee
43. Sri Lanka
44. Michael Atherton
45. Australia (1921)
46. Kepler Wessels
47. New Zealand
48. Wasim Akram, Imran Khan
49. West Indies
50. Allan Donald

Answers

Quiz 11

1. Essex
2. Pat Pocock
3. Six
4. Andy Flower
5. Dwayne Bravo
6. West Indies
7. Nixon McLean
8. Ricky Ponting
9. Durban
10. Mike Gatting
11. Nine years
12. Curtly Ambrose (14)
13. West Indies
14. The United Arab Emirates
15. West Indies
16. Michael Atherton
17. Derek Randall
18. Hashan Tillakaratne
19. Frank Worrell
20. India
21. India
22. Garry Sobers
23. Mushtaq Ahmed
24. Barry Richards
25. 26

26. 1995
27. Imran Khan
28. Ricky Ponting
29. Andy Roberts
30. Clem Hill
31. Derek Underwood
32. Old Trafford, Trent Bridge
33. The Melbourne Cricket Ground (MCG)
34. Chris Broad
35. Rahul Dravid
36. Bramall Lane
37. Sanath Jayasuriya
38. Australia
39. David Gower
40. Dermot Reeve
41. 1864
42. 1995
43. Arjuna Ranatunga
44. Zimbabwe
45. India
46. Andy Flower
47. Sachin Tendulkar
48. Gary Kirsten
49. Two
50. Sir Richard Hadlee

Quiz 12

1. Rodney Marsh
2. Geoff Boycott
3. Pakistan
4. The Nawab of Patudi Jr.
5. Riverside Stadium, Chester Le Street, Durham
6. Stephen Fleming
7. Dennis Lillee
8. Norman Gifford
9. 1987
10. Anil Kumble, Murali Kartik, Zaheer Khan
11. Garry Sobers
12. Sunil Gavaskar
13. Sir Jack Hobbs (12)
14. Sir Donald Bradman
15. Zimbabwe and Kenya
16. New Zealand
17. Sri Lanka
18. Dav Whatmore
19. Henry Olonga
20. Mohammad Azharuddin
21. WG Grace
22. Ian Botham
23. John Reid
24. April

25. Viv Richards
26. Scott Styris
27. 21
28. Zaheer Khan
29. Colin Cowdrey
30. Ashley Giles
31. Nottinghamshire
32. Alec Stewart
33. Aravinda de Silva
34. Ken Higgs, John Snow
35. Deryck Murray
36. Republic of Ireland
37. Richard Hadlee
38. Sir Donald Bradman
39. Kapil Dev
40. Andrew Flintoff
41. Adam Parore
42. David Shepherd
43. Chris Broad
44. Dennis Lillee
45. Chaminda Vaas
46. Canada
47. 39
48. Bob Taylor
49. Craig McDermott
50. Graham Gooch

Quiz 13

1. Andrew Hilditch
2. Guyana
3. Chaminda Vaas
4. Wasim Akram (18 years old)
5. Graham Gooch
6. Colin Croft
7. South Africa
8. A monsoon
9. 80
10. Four
11. Geoff Boycott, Wally Hammond, Colin Cowdrey
12. Sri Lanka
13. West Indies, Australia
14. Scotland, Kenya, Bangladesh
15. Sir Jack Hobbs
16. Eldine Baptiste
17. Sir Richard Hadlee
18. Michael Vaughan
19. Sunil Gavaskar, Mohammad Azharuddin
20. Courtney Walsh
21. 5,447
22. Keith Miller
23. Sourav Ganguly
24. Australia
25. Jacob Oram
26. Courtney Walsh
27. Five
28. Andrew Strauss and Robert Key
29. Shahid Afridi
30. Hedley Verity
31. Brendon McCullum
32. Dennis Lillee
33. Matthew Hayden, Jason Gillespie
34. Allan Border
35. Australia, West Indies
36. Colombo
37. Shane Warne
38. Three
39. Mohsin Khan
40. Max Walker
41. Alec Stewart
42. Zimbabwe
43. Zimbabwe
44. Ian Botham
45. False (none)
46. Joel Garner
47. Chris Broad
48. Four
49. Courtney Walsh
50. Lawrence Rowe

Quiz 14

1. Christchurch
2. Youngest
3. Courtney Walsh
4. 1996
5. Robin Jackman
6. Damien Martyn
7. Steve Bucknor
8. Sir Donald Bradman
9. Stephen Harmison
10. Inzamam-ul-Haq
11. Trevor Chappell
12. Clive Lloyd
13. Dominic Cork
14. Brian Close
15. Syed Kirmani
16. West Indies
17. Sri Lanka
18. Australia
19. Kapil Dev
20. Glenn McGrath
21. Mohammad Azharuddin
22. Australia
23. Sri Lanka
24. John Morris
25. Bill Woodfull
26. Ian Botham and Allan Lamb
27. Jack Russell
28. 15
29. Lawrence Rowe
30. England
31. Tiger
32. Jack Russell
33. Two
34. West Indies
35. Inzamam-ul-Haq
36. Graham Hick
37. Malcolm Marshall
38. Roy Dias
39. Fred Spofforth
40. Bangladesh
41. Nathan Astle
42. 23
43. Gundappa Viswanath
44. Five Years
45. Shane Warne
46. Marlon Samuels
47. Hampshire
48. South Africa
49. Old Trafford
50. 29 consecutive Test Match series

Quiz 15

1. 2004
2. Obstructing the field
3. Shoaib Akhtar
4. Mark Butcher
5. Alan Turner
6. Jeff Dujon
7. Sir Donald Bradman
8. India
9. None
10. South Africa
11. Jack Hobbs
12. Old Trafford
13. Allan Border
14. David Gower
15. David Boon, Allan Border, Ian Healy, Michael Slater, Mark Taylor
16. Hanif Mohammad
17. Pakistan
18. Hansie Cronje
19. Michael Gatting, David Gower, Nasser Hussein, Graham Gooch and Michael Atherton
20. Denis Compton
21. Zimbabwe
22. South Africa
23. Warwick Armstrong
24. New Zealand

25. Sir Garfield Sobers
26. Muttiah Muralitharan
27. Allan Border
28. Ricky Ponting
29. Fog
30. Arjuna Ranatunga
31. Ten
32. Inzamam-ul-Haq
33. Steve Waugh
34. Victor Trumper
35. Bishen Bedi
36. New Zealand (Richard Hadlee)
37. Tony Lock
38. Wilfred Rhodes
39. Andrew Flintoff
40. False
41. Barmy Army
42. Steve and Mark Waugh
43. Jim Troughton
44. 71 extras
45. Mike Gatting
46. Garry Sobers
47. Mark Waugh
48. Chris Old
49. Number Five
50. Gary Kirsten, Steve Waugh, Sachin Tendulkar

Quiz 16

1. South Africa
2. Nine
3. Curtly Ambrose
4. 1864
5. Johnny Briggs
6. Clive Lloyd (15)
7. Australia
8. Steve Waugh
9. 11am
10. Kenya
11. Dean Headley
12. Richie Benaud
13. Waqar Younis
14. Michael Holding
15. Jim Laker, David Steele
16. Muttiah Muralitharan
17. Richie Benaud
18. Wally Hammond
19. Russell Crowe
20. Viv Richards
21. Ali Bacher
22. Matthew Hayden
23. Bangladesh
24. Three
25. Everton Weekes, Frank Worrell and Clyde Walcott
26. Graham Gooch
27. Sir Donald Bradman
28. Sri Lanka, Bangladesh
29. 20 years
30. Marcus Trescothick
31. Old Trafford
32. 45 runs
33. Stephen Fleming
34. Headingley and Trent Bridge
35. Graham McKenzie
36. Ian Botham and Alan Knott
37. Richie Richardson
38. Seven
39. Hansie Cronje
40. Sachin Tendulkar
41. India
42. Allan Border
43. Sir Richard Hadlee
44. Basin Reserve, Wellington
45. Harare
46. Four
47. Kapil Dev
48. Sachin Tendulkar
49. New Zealand
50. Ian Healy

Answers

Quiz 17

1. WG Grace
2. Alec Bedser
3. Patsy Hendren
4. Shane Warne
5. Brian Lara
6. Garry Sobers
7. VVS Laxman
8. 14 years, 233 days
9. Ricky Ponting
10. Arjuna Ranatunga
11. South Africa
12. Gordon Greenidge
13. Alan Knott
14. West Indies
15. Chris Lewis
16. Eden Park
17. Alec and Eric Bedser
18. None
19. Graham Thorpe (24).
20. Twenty-one
21. Greg Chappell
22. Bobby Simpson
23. The Wanderers
24. Brian Lara
25. Marcus Trescothick
26. Bangladesh
27. Martin Crowe
28. 85 wickets
29. Andrew Flintoff, Nasser Hussain, Geraint Jones, Robert Key, Andrew Strauss, Graham Thorpe, Marcus Trescothick and Michael Vaughan
30. Mark Taylor
31. Pakistan, Zimbabwe
32. South Africa and Zimbabwe
33. Vinoo Mankad
34. Sir Richard Hadlee
35. 1975–76
36. West Indies
37. Sanath Jayasuriya
38. Sachin Tendulkar
39. United Arab Emirates
40. Nuwan Zoysa
41. Greg Chappell, Dennis Lillee
42. England
43. 29 batsmen
44. Mark Waugh
45. Abdul Qadir
46. Chris Gayle
47. Wasim Akram
48. Ridley Jacobs
49. Arnie Sidebottom
50. Rohan Kanhai

Quiz 18

1. Ian Healy
2. Hedley Verity
3. Dennis Lillee
4. Andy Bichel
5. Colin Cowdrey, Gordon Greenidge, Javed Miandad, Alec Stewart
6. Bowl a hat trick
7. New Zealand
8. 1993
9. Graham Gooch
10. 26
11. Neutral umpires stood
12. Wasim Akram
13. Lala Armarnath
14. Bishen Bedi
15. Sydney Cricket Ground (21)
16. 23
17. Pakistan (Hanif, Mushtaq and Sadiq Mohammad)
18. Allan Border and Sunil Gavaskar
19. Robert
20. Dennis Lillee
21. Curtly Ambrose
22. Steve Harmison
23. South Africa
24. Three
25. Riverside, Durham
26. Graham Dilley
27. Mark Butcher
28. West Indies
29. Australia
30. Merv Hughes
31. Phil Defreitas
32. Steve Waugh
33. Jason Gillespie, Andrew Caddick
34. Sunil Gavaskar
35. Garry Sobers
36. Lance Klusener
37. West Indies
38. Desmond Haynes
39. Chaminda Vaas
40. Graham Gooch
41. Australia
42. 1971
43. Anil Kumble
44. Ted Dexter
45. Chris Broad
46. Flower, Rennie, Strang
47. St Lucia
48. India
49. Courtney Walsh
50. Mark Boucher

Answers

Quiz 19

1. Harold 'Dickie' Bird
2. Sir Jack Hobbs
3. India
4. Muttiah Muralitharan
5. Mike Proctor
6. England, South Africa
7. Alfred Shaw
8. 365
9. Robin and Chris Smith
10. Michael Atherton
11. Kerry Packer
12. Victoria
13. Sri Lanka
14. Three
15. Lance Gibbs
16. Sri Lanka and South Africa
17. Durban
18. 21
19. Jermaine Lawson
20. ST Jayasuriya (340) & RS Mahanama (225)
21. George Headley (223 at age 20)
22. Graham Hick (141)
23. Adam Gilchrist
24. 87
25. Desmond Haynes
26. Sunil Gavaskar
27. Graham Yallop
28. Imran Khan
29. Mark Boucher
30. South African
31. Steve Waugh
32. Andrew Flintoff
33. Mohammad
34. Ian Botham
35. Sanath Jayasuriya
36. Allan Border
37. Lawrence Rowe
38. Viv Richards
39. Jack Russell
40. Australia
41. Zaheer Khan
42. Ten
43. Namibia
44. Sydney Barnes
45. Richard Illingworth
46. Alec Stewart
47. India
48. Angus Fraser
49. Virender Sehwag
50. Courtney Walsh (122 innings)

Quiz 20

1. Richie Benaud
2. West Indies
3. Denis Compton
4. Andrew Flintoff
5. Bangladesh
6. Virender Sehwag
7. The 1950s (1957)
8. Ashley Giles
9. Graeme Smith
10. Andrew Strauss, Andrew Flintoff
11. Michael Bevan
12. Shoaib Ahktar
13. 18th Century (1787)
14. Andrew Flintoff
15. Australia (Tasmania)
16. Michael Slater
17. Heath Streak
18. Graeme Smith
19. Rahul Dravid, Sachin Tendulkar
20. John Reid
21. Chetan Chauhan
22. Brian Lara
23. Shiverine Chanderpaul, Ramaresh Sarwan, Ryan Hinds
24. Brian Statham
25. Shane Warne
26. Brett Lee (85)
27. Waqar Younis
28. Makhaya Ntini
29. Dennis Lillee
30. Merv Dillon
31. Dennis Lillee and Rodney Marsh (95 wickets)
32. Wasim Akram
33. Allan Donald
34. Kapil Dev
35. Curtly Ambrose
36. Five
37. The eighth
38. 75
39. Gary Kirsten
40. The Melbourne Cricket Ground (MCG)
41. Sachin Tendulkar
42. Allan Lamb (13)
43. 17 years old
44. Sanath Jayasuriya
45. Gundappa Viswanath
46. Pakistan
47. Fred Trueman (86 wickets)
48. Angus Fraser
49. Four no balls
50. Heath Streak, Alistair Campbell, Andy Flower

Sticky Wicket

1. Arnie Sidebottom
2. Adam Gilchrist
3. Grant and Andy Flower, Ian and Greg Chappell
4. Rajesh Chauhan
5. Aravinda de Silva
6. Mahendra Nagamootoo
7. Arthur Dolphin
8. Aminul Islam
9. 'Ranji' (Kumar Shri Ranjitsinhji)
10. Buffalo Park
11. Denis Compton
12. Bert Oldfield
13. Sabina Park, Jamaica
14. Three, Shane Warne, Shane Bond and Shane Thomson
15. Sydney Barnes
16. Michael Vaughan
17. Javed Omar
18. Mike Gatting, John Emburey, Chris Cowdrey, Graham Gooch
19. Warwick Armstrong
20. Kumar Shri Duleepsinhji
21. Clarrie Grimmett
22. Wasim Akram
23. Inzamam-ul-Haq
24. Clem Hill
25. Junior Murray
26. Five
27. Duleep Mendis
28. Hedley Verity (8 times)
29. Fourteen
30. Two
31. Graham Roope
32. Philadelphia
33. Warwick Armstrong
34. Lawn bowls
35. Samuel Beckett
36. 35
37. Gary Gilmour
38. Keith Miller
39. Kumar Shri Ranjitsinhji
40. Martin Donnelly
41. The Nawab of Patudi
42. Elias
43. Marvin Atapattu
44. Mudassar Nazar
45. Geoff Allott
46. Merv Hughes
47. 1983
48. Nilesh Kulkarni
49. Cyril Washbrook
50. 19